P9-AOK-273

Nicholas Ruddock, Alex Leslie & Jeff Park

PS
8329
C65
2009

COMING ATTRACTIONS
09

The publishers acknowledge the support of the Canada Council for the Arts, the Government of Ontario through the Ontario Media Development Corporation and the Government of Canada through the Book Publishing Industry Development Program for their publishing activities.

"Sebald" by Nicholas Ruddock was first published in *Exile*. "How Eunice Got Her Baby" by Nicholas Ruddock first appeared in *The Fiddlehead* and *Journey Prize Stories 19*, and was made into a film by the Canadian Film Centre. "After Butterpot" by Nicholas Ruddock originally appeared in *The Antigonish Review*. "Ghost Stories" by Alex Leslie was first published in *The Fiddlehead*. "Swimmers" by Alex Leslie first appeared on Joyland.ca. "Preservation" by Alex Leslie was first published in *enRoute*, and won a CBC Literary Award. "Back to Disney," "A Boat in Still Water" and "Ain't Gonna Be Your Dog" by Jeff Park originally appeared in *The Fiddlehead*.

ISBN 978 0 7780 1337 2 (hardcover)
ISBN 978 0 7780 1338 9 (softcover)

Cover art from Art Goût Beauté, 1922
Book design by Michael Macklem

Printed in Canada

PUBLISHED IN CANADA BY OBERON PRESS

Canada Council   Conseil des Arts
for the Arts   du Canada

Contents

INTRODUCTION

Welcome to this collection's wild worlds and wild words, as etched by three fine new writers, Nicholas Ruddock, Alex Leslie and Jeff Park.

Nicholas Ruddock writes fiction and poetry in Guelph, but has spent time in the Yukon and Newfoundland, and this is reflected in his accomplished work, which delves into sexual liaisons and conception and abortion and childbirth and very slow robberies. He expertly handles small-town Canadiana, but there is also a European sensibility to some of his work, especially a story like "Sebald." His novel, *The Parabolist*, will be published by Doubleday in 2010.

Alex Leslie lives in Vancouver and writes fine stories and essays of the west coast, often set in remote valleys and logging roads of Vancouver Island, stories dealing with family histories and fissures and geology and music and natural disasters. They read like a new form of ghost story. Her impressive fiction and non-fiction has been much published recently, in *The Fiddlehead, Descant, Event, Prairie Fire, Best Canadian Stories*, and in Air Canada's *enRoute* magazine, after winning a CBC Literary Award. She is working on a collection of stories and a novella.

Jeff Park writes fiction and poetry and drama. His pointed stories boast wildly varying voices, subjects and settings, from a wintry marijuana grow-op to skewed romances to do with Mystic Pizza and an atomic submarine and hustlers and dogs and sex and chaos. I really like them. He has spent time at the Banff Centre, teaches at the University of Saskatchewan in Saskatoon, and roams the steppes listening to Howlin' Wolf.

MARK ANTHONY JARMAN

Contributions for Coming Attractions 10, *published or unpublished, should be sent to Oberon Press, 205–145 Spruce Street, Ottawa, Ontario K1R 6P1 before 31 March, 2010. All manuscripts should enclose a stamped self-addressed envelope.*

NICHOLAS RUDDOCK

Sebald

Late one afternoon, in the autumn of the year 2001, in Guelph, Ontario, when the trees were still clinging to their red and yellow leaves and the sun was setting behind the church—it cast a shadow darkening down to the river—I came face to face with the Anglo-German writer, W. G. Sebald. He stood alone on the southeast corner of Macdonell and Wyndham, apparently studying a map. At his feet was a large battered leather valise, of the type that predated the tyranny of the airport carousel; its corners were not rounded but right-angled, and protected by brass fittings. I recognized him at once, for his face was turned down and to the right, mimicking exactly, as it were, the black-and-white photograph that appeared on the inner flap, back cover, of my copy of *Austerlitz*.

He was a man of medium height, his face preternaturally pale. I well knew his obsessive habit (or, to be more exact, the obsessive habit of his protagonists) of walking disconsolately, incessantly, as if in a trance, through fog, through rain, and through the polluted mists of post-industrial cities. In his novels, these restless urban meanderings appeared to be aimless, yet they were driven by some vague personal malaise. They ended, for no particular reason, in railway stations, or in cathedrals, in museums, in near-empty cafes, or in the nondescript threadbare flats of distant and damaged friends, all in pursuit of an understanding of sorts, an understanding which, I confess, often eluded me, and which left both of us, protagonist and reader, mesmerized, in a strange dichotomy of energized torpor. What was he doing here, in Guelph? As many photographs taken at that time will attest, including the one in *Austerlitz*, Sebald's eyes were sunken deeply into his face. They appeared bruised, as if his haunted pursuit of recent history had brought him face to face with the spirit of evil, or, worse, with that of complacency, cowardice and calumny. All of these thoughts raced through me as soon as I saw him. I observed him more closely. He had a thick moustache, salt-white, on his upper lip. I have often observed that intellectuals have little interest in self-grooming, that they finish with shaving and indeed with all personal care when only part-way through the task. Perhaps they fear haemorrhage from the inattentive razor. Perhaps their minds are simply pre-occupied with greater concerns. At any rate, on this occasion, the unmistakeable Sebald was quite neatly dressed, with a grey overcoat buttoned tightly to his neck, and his sparse hair was bent hither and yon by a particularly unrelenting wind. His posture, stooped from fatigue, reflected, I thought later, his having borne upon his shoulders the cumulative moral weight of Western Europe for a lifetime, and from having borne it in such a personal, painful, and much-documented way. His presence here was a mystery, a tantalizing one.

I felt, from the manner in which he stood there alone with his map, his suitcase at his feet, that I should intercede. Never once, I have to mention, in the course of the next few hours, did I admit to recognizing him, nor did I acknowledge his fame, his written work, his teaching, nor in any way did I allude (except indirectly) to his fictional world of family loss, forced emigration, emotional numbness, personal abnegation, violence, politics, art or architecture, other than in response to the information he offered me. Nor did I refer to him as anything other than "Wilhelm Sechelt," the name he presented, strangely, as his. Nor, upon my cautious approach on that corner and on that afternoon, and upon his asking my name, did I respond truthfully either; I gave my surname as "Weiss," which is not my own. I did this not out of any need for subterfuge, but instead to give a perfect balance to our imperfect, yet for me momentous, relationship. I felt that my life had been so trivial by comparison with his that I was marked, as if in crimson, by failure. The change of surname I wrought for myself, at that moment, the name which sprang unbidden from what must have been an unacknowledged void in my soul, seemed, as I said it: "Weiss," that it could bring about for me a release, as if I could step out from myself into his more profound, more potent world.

I stopped by his side.

"Can I help you?" I said.

"Yes thank you, I'm looking for the Park Mall."

How reticent he was when he spoke! The lengthy, accumulating sentences for which he was renowned in his novels were nowhere in evidence. There were no mesmerizing digressions, no thought-provoking reversals, no melancholic stops, no discursive subordinate clauses, no seemingly effortless interlinking of thought with hindered or obstructed emotion. Yet the absence of these features did not concern me in any way, nor did it make me doubt to whom I spoke. In fact, I accepted his spare elocution as even further evidence of his identity, for a writer of such eloquence must, in his private moments and his personal interactions, seek a relatively brutal simplicity of expression.

He shifted the suitcase at his feet as if to protect it. I saw, with a glance, that it was much abraded by age and by heavy usage. Inside it, I was certain, could be found a meticulous yet unfinished manuscript, jottings for poetry, and ordinary memorabilia of the sort collected by any tourist: postcards, ticket stubs, receipts. These everyday items, I knew, he squirrelled away, later to reproduce within the pages of his work, where they lent a spurious reality to the convolutions of his dense prose. A postcard here, a thin drawing there, an amateur snapshot, a poor reproduction of a Renaissance painting, a distant view of a bridge or of smoke spilling from an assortment of ominous chimneys in an evening sky: these were the sort of souvenirs he chose, with his peculiar sensibility, to illuminate his themes. What could he find here, in our humble city? How I longed for the privilege of viewing the contents of his valise.

I caught myself in the midst of that thought, and replied,

"The Park Mall?"

Even as the words left my lips, I found myself dreaming of somehow attaching myself to him in some inconspicuous way. I could be, to him, a Rosencrantz, a Guildenstern, a Charles Kinbote, a footnote in his yet-to-be-contemplated approved biography, on the bottom, say, of page 673 (the page number I confess came to me later). There, I hoped, in that footnote, a discerning reader in years hence would find me masquerading as this certain "Mr. Weiss," a minor but critical cog in the drive-wheel of the locomotive of his genius. A reticent man who briefly guided him on his journey through Southern Ontario. A man who could be seen, to extend the metaphor I have chosen, as a mere caboose on the writer's train, were that not presumptuous, or as a lowly cattle-car (perish that image) or even (what was I thinking?) a suicide who threw himself upon the tracks in front of the engine as Sebald left Guelph bound for Kitchener, and so, in that self-destructive act, stopped the great writer, there in the railway carriage, ever so briefly.

I re-entered the conversation already in progress.

"The Park Mall?" I said again. This time I threw an inflection into my voice to betray my surprise. For, of all our local buildings, the Park "Mall"—it was not a mall but an apartment building of thirteen stories festooned with rusted balconies and bristling, on its flat head, with communication towers—was well-known locally as a "blot on the landscape." This was the phrase most used by writers of letters-to-the-editor to our local newspaper, letters which bemoaned the deterioration, in spirit and edifice, of our small community. In winter, moreover, this same building became, if not the source then the vector of a wind so powerful that it seized upon the elderly who, having been forced out by necessity upon the small winter errands that sustained them within their meagre apartments, were then hurled from their feet in astounding numbers. They fell down helpless upon the ice and snow, fracturing hips and wrists brittled with age. Then

13

came the ambulances, their sirens reverberating up against the surrounding walls, while in the background scraps of discarded paper, thrown high by those same unforgiving winds, twirled wildly.

"The Park Mall?"

I was too shy, so all I did was stand there, and I waited for his next words.

"The Park Mall, yes, please," he said.

"I'll take you there," I said, "it's on my way."

I was in a state of some anxiety, diaphoretic and even euphoric, due to my unusual proximity to greatness, and due also to my determined effort to hide, from my companion, any outward sign of nervous tension. I tightly gripped my hands into fists within my coat pockets. An independent observer, following close behind us and with a ready ear, would have found our conversation to be casual to the extreme. As we walked, I pointed out to Sebald the landmarks I felt would pique his curiosity, or reverberate with his known written concerns, or harmonize with the tenor of his melancholy. There, high on that hill, I pointed out, is the Church of our Lady, modelled exactly after the cathedral at Rheims in France, so that it is, here in Guelph, a duplicate in miniature, yet still large enough to overwhelm the skyline in a very European way. Established here in 1877, it was by necessity built in stages and, through some historical quirk that confuses me even today, its foundation was partially paid for by the Emperor Maximilian of Mexico, a man of some curiosity who was later immortalized, at the moment of his death by firing-squad, in a painting by Edouard Manet. Incidentally, I also said, how telling it is that our cathedral, high upon this hill, is an exact copy of a Colonial Power cathedral. As if our imagination, here in Canada, was as empty, at that time, as a Cree or Huron or Iroquoian village after the purposeful introduction, by our ancestors, of smallpox.

"May I take your bag?" I asked.

14

"No," he said.

And here, I continued as we walked along together, if you don't mind a short but scenic detour on the way to the Park Mall, follow me down to our river as it passes under the Gordon Street bridge. Ah, here it is: a historic plaque such as one might see in Nurnberg or Dusseldorf or Rotterdam or Manchester or Dresden or München, a blue and gold metallic script emblazoned on a heraldic shield atop a pole planted firmly in the ground, in the corner of a park which has, within it, a low wooden structure serving tea and ice cream. On this plaque—I pointed to it—is written of the unexpected arrival here, in 1827, of several hundred Scots, by way, believe it or not, of Venezuela. There, they had been subjected to misfortune in the form of malaria, yellow fever, starvation, and the poisoned arrows of a native population less acquiescent than ours. Therefore they had fled from that less than salubrious country and, not being welcome in the United States, they had struggled here to Upper Canada, by sea, by foot and by cart overland, destitute, starving and ridden with disease; half of these Scots, mind you, were women and small children. I could see Sebald's curiosity was stimulated by this story, so I was encouraged to continue and also encouraged, again, to draw parallels between this emigration of ours and similar events in his own fiction. (My motive, I admit, was again to cast myself in his eyes as a person to whom he could relate as an equal. A preposterous motive, in retrospect.)

At any rate, I said to my new acquaintance as we stood by that plaque, while behind us the shouts of frisbee-players and small children on swings echoed through the chill but welcoming air, imagine the situation faced then by the settlers already here in Guelph, engaged in carving a precarious living out of primeval wilderness! How seldom, I emphasized, can we tell such a satisfying story—at this I looked carefully at my friend—for, as the script in blue and gold proclaimed, these refugees were taken in and cared for despite shortages of grain and berries and root vegetables, thus visiting a winter's hardship upon all, settlers and immigrants alike. What a contrast that behaviour was, I pointed out—and I lowered the register of my voice significantly as I did so—to the conduct in 1939 of the Canadian Government which turned back, to the concentration camps of the Continent, a boatload of 907 Jewish refugees, again mostly women and small children aboard the ill-fated vessel *St. Louis*, all shunned as pariah at the gates of our democracy. They were returned to certain death. This heartlessness, I said to Sebald, went unregistered by our parents and by our grandparents, for our government swept its wicked broom for us, leaving us at arms-length, as did—here I looked at him directly—the Nazi government for its citizens, who were equally unaware, apparently, of Auschwitz and Buchenwald, even as they themselves produced, transported, and unpacked the gas crystals of Zyklon B.

Sebald looked at his watch. "The Park Mall, Mr. Weiss," he said, "where is it, exactly, from here?"

I pointed north. "There," I said, "let's go."

I could tell, despite his taciturn response to my observations, that he was deeply moved, for he wiped his eyes with a handkerchief and pretended, to me, that it was naught but the wind, now freshening even more. So we turned our steps and soon, at last, we were at the Park Mall itself. It was no surprise to me that an ambulance stood at the front entrance. The attendants were carrying out, on a stretcher, a thin woman with wispy hair who appeared to be having breathing difficulties. She had nothing on but a shabby housecoat and, on her legs, thick brown stockings that had fallen to the ankles. Sebald looked at these stockings with compassion, as if they were a metaphor. Many of the lodgers here, I explained, are seniors on threadbare pensions. Many of them are widowed, and many, as we cast a look together at the list of names behind the glass in the outer lobby, once were refugees from post-war Europe. There are Dutch and Poles,

Hungarians and Yugoslavians, and Ukrainians, I said, who have lived through times so horrifyingly unimaginable that they are now close-lipped and reticent, their English torn and thick-tongued, their names riddled with c's and z's and v's and w's. Knowing Sebald as I thought I did, I expected him to reach up with his index finger and press the black button beside one of those obscure and jumbled names, but instead he hesitated only briefly while he scanned the directory and then he pressed "John Cole," a name so simple that it startled me, until I remembered the patronizing habit of our immigration officers who, upon registering the arrival in Canada of a Schewtschenko or a Kolodziejczak, would coolly print their names as Smith and Cole. And Smith and Cole they would be, officially, for the rest of their days, as if they had never otherwise lived and breathed upon the planet Earth.

"Yes who is it?" came a man's voice through the intercom.

"It is I," said Sebald, and with that simple statement, I once more felt a rush of certainty, as I had when I first recognized him. Who but a literary man whose first language is not English, but who has lived in the English language for half a lifetime, would use the first-person singular pronoun in the subjective case in such an exacting manner? With this thought in mind, and as the buzz came that would usher him into the inner sanctum of the Park Mall, thus removing him from my life and my influence forever, I felt panic. I broke out in a cold sweat. I leaned against the lobby door even as it made its raucous welcome. Sebald looked at me carefully and, for the first time, with evident concern.

"Are you all right?" he said.

I staggered and placed my palm on the wall to stabilize myself. I felt my eyes move rapidly of their own volition, spinning, as if searching for an inner fulcrum upon which they could grip and thus find a tenuous balance. In retrospect, this spontaneous episode of dysphoria must have sprung unbidden from my own subconscious. Out came a

17

spontaneous expulsive moan from my throat and lips, producing, at that exact moment, the one potent word that meant more to W. G. Sebald than any other word in our mutually shared language.

"Vertigo!"[1] I said.

Sebald, startled, looked outside. The ambulance was pulling away.

"*Haben Sie warme Socken?*" he said. I was astonished to hear these words from his lips, for of course they were meaningless to me.[2]

"Do you speak German?" he said.

"No."

"Come with me, you do not look well."

Thus we rode the elevator to the seventh floor, where, from the end of the hallway, a view could be obtained of the southern reaches of the city, stretching out beyond the checker-board houses of suburbia to the once-verdant, now autumnal fields of corn, grain, cattle, and the soft Ontario hillsides interspersed with woodlots all the way to the horizon.

"What a sight," I said, already feeling much better, "Why look, I can see the roof of my own home, one of the oldest in the city. Notice the stonework, the unique parapet design, the...."

"Here we are," he said, again dismissing my observations without comment.

He knocked quickly yet quietly on the door of number 77, and it opened. A short, bald, solidly built man of at least 75 years embraced my companion immediately, as if they had not met in decades, as if they had once shared an experience of such intensity that all reserve, upon meeting, was thrown

---

1 "Vertigo," by W.G. Sebald, translation by Michael Hulse, New Directions, 1999

2 I committed to memory the phonetics of Sebald's utterance and repeated them later to a native German speaker. His translation was, simply: "Do you have warm socks?"

to the wind. Awkwardly, I waited. An elderly woman appeared from within the apartment. There was a heavy pall of cigarette smoke in the air. Then the door clicked behind us and the chain was, unusually, I felt, for that hour of the day, fastened by Sebald himself and then, as if to add further to the air of intrigue brought about by that secretive movement, I noticed that all the windows within the apartment were obscured by the thickest of curtains, heavy black floor-length shrouds that blotted out the day as if it were a pestilence. At night, I realized, these curtains must be entirely impervious to streetlight. Then I was introduced to John Cole and to his wife, whose name was given to me as "Izabella," and the two men retired from the hallway, where first we stood, to what must have been the dining-room, still half-visible to me. There they began an animated conversation in German—that much I could recognize—and my impression was that my friend Sebald was of course fluent in that language, whereas Mr. Cole was hesitant and not a native speaker. This impression gained strength when, upon sitting in the kitchen with Izabella, to whom I had obviously been seconded, I observed a framed photograph on the kitchen wall depicting, unmistakeably, a view of the Danube River as it flowed through Budapest. There was the dome of the Parliament Buildings barely visible through the fog rising from the eerily still surface of the water. I thought I could detect a feathering of snow upon the iron railing that the photographer had chosen to angulate through the foreground. These observations I kept to myself, as now I faced the bright eyes of Frau Izabella Cole, a woman whose intensity of gaze and speech was so pronounced that I immediately fell under her spell as if hypnotized. So sharp and intrusive, even demanding, were her queries, and so unusual her appearance, that I was taken aback and lost all auditory contact with the men in the adjoining room. For Izabella Cole, despite having the pallor one might expect from living within such stifling quarters, had eyes so dark that I could not help but think that she had Roma blood. These eyes smouldered with such interest in me that, even though I felt that some of her passion may have been feigned, or exaggerated, I was alarmed nevertheless and forced to think rapidly, as if once again I were a student, nerve-wracked, facing an oral examination of great import. She wore, upon her head, a wig of thick curly hair, ash-blonde in colour, that had slipped down upon her waxen forehead until it lay near-contiguous to her eyebrows. This lent her, I felt, a primitive ferocity. Moreover, further carelessness on her part (or so I assumed) had allowed the rubberized lower edge of this hairpiece to be easily visible, and so I found her, as who would not, a disturbing cross, visually, between a clown and a ferret with the gift of tongues. Moreover, she smoked cigarettes voraciously. Smoke streamed not only from her mouth and nostrils but also, curiously, from her right ear. I later spoke to a medical friend who informed me that, indeed, such an oddity is anatomically possible, provided that the eardrum on the affected side has a perforation, often a chronic condition of those raised in poverty.

"Weiss!" she said, "where did you get that name!"

"From my parents," was my reply, and then I was forced to rapidly fabricate such a flimsy ladder of falsehoods that, had Sebald and John Cole not rescued me by keeping their meeting to but a quarter-hour, I would have toppled from my fictitious history to the ground, there to be cushioned only by the unsubstantial bodies of my imaginary parents and grandparents, God Rest their Souls.

"Where was your mother born?"

"Did you have books?"

"Did you have a horse?"

"When did you develop that nasty shaking? Does it run in your family?"

"What do you put on your *Kartoffeln*[3]?"

I squirmed under her scrutiny. My rudimentary knowl-

3 "potatoes"

20

edge of middle-European geography, gleaned from an atlas years ago, was strained so far past belief that, on one occasion, when I was forced to describe the streetscape and the country in which my phantom grandfather worked as a phantom shoemaker, Izabella briefly choked with laughter upon the smoke that otherwise spilled from her effortlessly. I feared she would unmask me, or mock me with scorn or disgust, and then disclose my subterfuge to Sebald himself.

But "Tell me more, tell me more!" It seemed, I felt later, when I had time to re-examine the events of that evening, that the two of us, Izabella and I, had somehow shared a secret, that we had bonded, co-conspirators within my own extemporaneous and ill-thought fiction. And then, I thought, perhaps she had spent her life surrounded by many such fictions, that such fabrications and reinterpretations were so commonplace to her that they were just as real as any sworn truth. By contrast, novices such as I, when we conjured false history, withered inside. Worms of guilt took their inevitable toll. These were my thoughts at a later hour, for at the time I was far too awhirl in my emotions to have rational thoughts. My horse, I told her, had been named Canto, and that Italian word bubbled up from some heretofore-forgotten cauldron of stewed European romance.

"Canto," she said, "how lovely."

Sebald suddenly re-appeared through the haze in the kitchen and took me by the elbow. He observed that my vertigo had obviously passed, to which I agreed.

"The train west then," he said, "at 6.50."

I shook hands, first with John Cole and then with Izabella herself. Her left eye twitched at me, or winked. I held her hand longer than was absolutely necessary, as indeed she held mine in reciprocation. Sebald and I left. As we stepped out onto Yarmouth Street, now in darkness, I looked across the street at the Public Library, where I had spent so many hours in my youth.

"Look, Mr Sechelt,' I said, "look over there."

I continued to call him "Sechelt," of course, because I was determined to accept that masquerade of his, determined not to challenge him, or to strip away any disguise he had chosen to assume. Nevertheless, knowing his interest in public buildings, and particularly his interest in libraries, I could not let this opportunity pass. I took the right arm of his coat between my fingers and thus stopped him briefly. I turned him to the west. Once again, I assumed a professorial voice so as better to impress him, though certainly my success so far in that regard had been limited. I pointed out that over there, where now stands a tediously nondescript glass-and-brick edifice, once stood a remarkable example of a Carnegie Library. It had been, in its day, an imposing neo-Classic design of artificial stone, complete with sham pillars reminiscent of the Acropolis. That now-destroyed building, I stated to Sebald, who seemed a bit restless as I spoke, served as our intellectual nerve centre here in Guelph for six decades, despite being opposed, during its construction, by unionists who felt, not without cause, that American "blood money," via the Carnegie family, would forever taint the purity of the Library's stated purpose.

However, as before, nothing I said seemed to affect him.

"The train," he said.

I walked him to the railroad station, where I said nothing about its architectural significance. I watched him purchase a ticket. He paid with cash. Then we stood outside and, within a minute, the bright light of the train from Toronto curved from the east into view, and we bade farewell. I can still feel the power of his grip, and I had to resist the temptation to embrace him. He boarded the train.

Suddenly, from the upper steps, he turned to me and shouted, "My valise! Inside!"

The train had already begun to move. I turned and ran, my heart pounding from the enormity of my mission. There it was, as forlorn and forgotten as any child, under the ledge at the ticket window. I grasped it by its worn handle and ran back outside. Already the train was rolling, slowly, slowly westwards, and Sebald was aboard, turning toward me from the top of the carriage-way. He beckoned me on, desperately. I sprinted. I reached upwards. Then, to my horror, I tripped on the uneven surface and I fell, and the suitcase hit the concrete and catapulted under the wheels of the accelerating train. He saw it all. I heard him cry out and I saw his travelling case split wide-open by the iron flange of a rolling wheel, inches from my head. The contents burst out upon the platform.

Socks, stockings and pantyhose flew everywhere. There were brown ones, white ones, short and calf-length and knee-high, hose of all sorts torn and tossed hither and yon by the slipstream of the train. There were even black fishnet stockings coiled like snakes. I lay there and then I rose up and retrieved the case, which was lying, severed in two, the top torn from the bottom and twisted askew on the weeds between the tracks. The train receded west to Kitchener. I was left standing with the shattered remains of his luggage, with blood congealing on the knuckles of my right hand from its sudden contact with the concrete of the platform.

I never saw him again.

Sechelt, he had called himself.

When he died on 14 December 2001—a car accident in East Anglia—there was his photograph in the newspaper, unmistakeably him, morose, ironic, and as real as if he were standing beside me on that windswept afternoon. Oh for his spirit of restlessness, I thought. It was not for me to question his reasons for carrying a valise full of stockings. Even the most mundane object can harbour within it a significance not readily perceived by the untutored heart.

My life resumed its uneventful course. I found myself unable to shake the memory of his visit. I found myself thinking about the Coles living in their darkness, their apartment shuttered as if at war. I wondered about his connection to them. I was far too shy, too ashamed of my previous misrepresentation to ever approach the Coles again. I began to experience a recurrent dream which was in no way frightening, but which often woke me in the middle of the night. I saw W.G. Sebald down on his knees in the kitchen, measuring Izabella Cole's leg from ankle to knee with tailor's tape. Then he began to sift through the samples in his valise, as if in fact he believed that one could be superior to the next. She took a long draught on her cigarette, exhaled, and smoke drifted from her damaged ear. They laughed secretively. Sebald dropped the stockings as if his task was impossible and he sat down on the floor, his back against the cupboard.

Some day, I thought, I would seek expiation for the disguise I had assumed on that day.

As it was, however, I waited too long. John Cole died first—I saw the notice in the paper, a notice with no adornment at all—and then, not too long ago, while passing the Park Mall on a winter's morning, I saw an ambulance waiting there again. This time, attached to nasal prongs of oxygen, Izabella Cole herself was lying there on a stretcher, her hairpiece low, now tilted on her head like a ragged fez. As the stretcher passed, she looked up and, despite her physical discomfort, her gasps for air, she spied me and held up her hand, as if to stop all proceedings.

"Weiss," she said, "Weiss!"

My heart pounded in my chest. Before my words came, her attendants suddenly formed a wall of blue. The ambulance doors opened and closed and she was swept away down Yarmouth Street. Possibly the last words she uttered on this earth were, unknown to her, false: "Weiss," she had said. A stranger's name upon her lips.

Morbid sensitivity is not exclusively the curse of artists. It lives in me. In fact, I comprehended after Sebald left, it lives in us all, embryonic, waiting for something external, a catalyst to either stifle it into hardness or quicken it like a pulse, to torture or thrill.

I should have showed him more when he was here. We

could have walked to the river together. I could have, that very same night, showed him the breath of fog like a shroud moving up the hill, climbing and rolling over the stone wall which surrounds the house, now a historic site empty after dusk, the house of our famous poet.

In Flanders' fields the poppies blow.

Sebald and I could have stepped carefully into that autumnal garden, where everything lies dead, dried-out, sered and angulated. We could have remembered the sheer depressive weight he had felt upon his shoulders once in Venice, the near-catatonia, and then, finally, the compulsive travelling that drove him by foot, by train, by sea, to circle the heart of his despair.

"The larks still bravely singing fly," I would have said.

We could have agreed on that, the two of us, no matter who he was.

How Eunice Got Her Baby

Eunice didn't get her baby in the usual way, through sexual intercourse with a boy in a bed, in a car, or out on the meadow after dark. Instead, she inherited her baby from the estate of her older sister Florence, through a tragedy. From the estate? Well, it wasn't really an estate, because of course there was no will made up, but when the baby became available, through the sudden accident that claimed the life of Florence, it was Eunice who was first in line. And that was a proper thing as it turned out, because Eunice was the best mother a baby could have. Better than the natural mother, some said, because Florence had a wild way about her that Eunice didn't have. Flo was impulsive and did things on a dare. Flo drove down the Trans-Canada Highway on the blackest night of the year with all the car-lights turned off so she could see the stars better. Flo shut her eyes, or pretended to shut her eyes, and she crossed the busiest streets like that, with her arms stretched out.

Look at me, she said, I'm a zombie.

She also drank way too many beers too early on at dances, then right away she'd dance too close, and stay out way too late, past the wee hours. She'd skip classes at school the next day too, including the ones on precautions, and how she got her baby was therefore no mystery to any of her friends. Why, more often than not, Flo came home with her underpants scrunched up in her purse. That was Flo, but that was not Eunice, and that's how her little baby, Pasquena, who we all called Queenie, got lucky, sort of, when tragedy struck her mother down.

Now let's not go on too much about the wild side of Flo. There was lots that was good about her. She's got energy to burn, that's what her father said whenever he was asked. She's got her thermostat cranked up high. Her father talked like that because he had one of the best jobs on the whole

Southern Shore, and that involved fuel oil. He had a yellow truck everybody recognized, and he knew everything there was to know about thermostats, and energy, and the foolish waste of heat. Some families burned their oil up twice as fast as others, he'd seen that over and over. And Flo? Well, Flo, she's like a comet, he said, there's no stopping Flo. She's fire in the sky. She burns oil. She was the oldest of all the seven children, the first in line, the experimental one, and Eunice was the baby, the last of the whole family. That meant, praise the Lord, that Eunice got insulated from the wild side of Flo by nine whole years, and all she knew about Flo was the love and the care she got from the only sister she had. Eunice always got a kiss, nothing less, no matter how late Flo got home, no matter how scrunched up Flo's underpants might have been, pushed into the top of her purse just a half-hour before. Eunice got the kisses, but she never dreamed she'd get a baby from Flo. If she'd ever dreamed that, it would have been a nightmare. There's not too many good ways you can inherit a baby.

Even with Flo being the way she was, everything would have been fine if it hadn't been for the boy she met. His name was Darryl Bugden, and though he had lots of charms and attributes attractive to a girl, he also had the heart and the spirit of a criminal born. Not just one who picked it up along the way, for a lark with friends, but one born right to it from the word go.

How'd it happen? Flo was at the Minimart, the one she worked at on Long's Hill, reading a magazine and sitting by the cash, when she was introduced to Darryl. There was no-one else in the store. It was 8 PM, three hours to go before she closed up against the scattered few customers who came in. It was mostly cigarettes and chips and the furtive magazines for total losers, that's all.

This here's a stick-up, was what Darryl said, his first words to her.

Flo looked up and there he was, six foot four at least, with dark curly hair and a smile despite what he said to her. All those teeth were perfect. What's with that, she thought, perfect teeth? That's rare. He did not look threatening to Flo, but how could she know, that death would appear to her in this outfit, those teeth, those words she'd only heard on TV? It never occurred to her, and it never would have occurred to anyone, looking at that smile. Anyway, it sure didn't happen right away, it took three years.

A stick-up? she said.

When she got the job, the boss said to her, if someone comes in and says, This is a Stick-up, then you just collapse to the floor in a dead faint. Piss your pants too, that's the best. Make as big a mess as you can and breathe like you're a spastic on the verge of a fit. Oftentimes they'll just say, Jesus Christ!, and run out of the store and go somewhere else.

Somehow the boss had figured that out on his own, from what happened to him once. He didn't plan it, it just happened to him and it worked. He sure didn't get that advice out of the manual that came to all the new employees, from the Downtown Merchants. In that manual, it said, just hand over all the money, wordless, and do not put up any resistance. Most of these robbers are on drugs and they're twitchy, unpredictable.

It was the nice smile he had that kept her sitting there. There was no way she was going to fall to the floor and do the rest of that whole crazy drill. How bad could a girl look, no matter when?

There's no money here. Everything bigger than a five goes right down that slot, she said.

She pointed to the wall behind her.

Straight down into the safe.

Actually it was a slot in the wall that went straight into a cardboard liquor box that was on top of the safe. She could see it in her mind's eye, sitting there full of loose money spilling over the sides. The boss long ago forgot the number to the safe so this was a money bypass. It's a trick, he said, that fools most of them all the time.

The safe, the combination is unknown to me, she said.

He smiled some more but he just stood there.

The walls are three feet thick, and solid iron.

The next thing Darryl did was get over the counter. He suddenly turned and slid his butt over the plexiglass that lay over top of the lottery tickets, and there he was, he twisted around and his feet landed on the floor right beside Flo. They stood there like a couple. She got scared then, and looked out the door. Maybe there'd be a customer to come in and save her, but that was not likely, maybe the old man with the cane or the fat lady for bubble gum, but what chance of that? There was no-one in sight. And what chance would they have, anyway? None, she figured.

Lay down on the floor, he said. Those were the next words he had with the love of his life.

Down went Flo onto the linoleum. The tiles were lifted here and there, swept just once a week so they didn't raise the dust, and she knew her white blouse, the one she bought with her own money, the one she never should have worn that night, would be ruined. Thank God for the old jeans she had on. Maybe she'd be dead soon enough anyway. It wouldn't matter then what she had on, unless there was a picture in the paper. They didn't usually show dead bodies. Even then, so what? Flo didn't care about that really. Then she lost her nerve all at once.

There there, don't cry, said Darryl, just shut up.

Then Darryl took his left foot and laid it down on Flo's chest near her throat while she lay there in the dirt. It was a boot like a cowboy might have, with a heel like iron maybe two inches long.

I'm now the man at the cash tonight, he said.

He pressed his foot on her throat some, but she could still breathe.

Don't you say a word or move, he said, or I'll stomp on your windpipe with the toe of this boot. They got steel toes.

29

There was a tinkle from the door bell and she heard the shuffle-shuffle of the old man with the cane. Eight-fifteen on the button every night, for the newspaper and the dog food. Once the boss saw that the old man always got dog food, he'd marked up the cans to $2.00 for each and every one. The old guy will never notice that, he said, the old goat, the old geezer, the old fool. Later, Flo changed it back to $1.25 with the rotating stamp. The boss'll never notice that, she said, the old miser. That was the general atmosphere at the Minimart, so Darryl there behind the counter, his foot on Flo's throat, didn't really change things all that much.

Where's Flo? said the old man when he came up to pay.

Underfoot somewhere, maybe in the back, said Darryl bold as brass, I'm on the cash tonight. For all I know, she's lying down somewhere.

That's how the rest of the night was with Darryl. Flo lay on the floor but she couldn't cry anymore. Darryl took in all the cash and put none of it down the slot. After an hour went by, Darryl took off his boots with the steel toes, and just pressed on her neck with his stocking foot. She was surprised, the sock smelled clean, like wool. Whenever she looked up, he still had on that smile which never changed. He thought he was a smart-ass, she could tell, but that was common enough in all the men she knew. By 9.30, she no longer trembled but Darryl was none too happy with the lousy take of, so-far, $38.50.

This is one slow store, Darryl said.

That foot of his seemed to move further down from her throat, down her chest until it was right on the top of her left breast. She shifted down a bit.

Not a lot of money comes in to this dumb store, he said.

Watch that foot please, said Flo.

Sorry, said Darryl. He released a bit of pressure but he didn't shift the toes at all. Is that better?

That's better, said Flo, but in the quiet times, between the customers, Flo thought she could feel that foot getting rhythmic on her chest. Oh well, just lay there, she figured, let it go.

I might just close up early, said Darryl at 10.30.

Leave now, said Flo, there's an idea.

Then what do I do with you? said Darryl.

Me? said Flo.

You're the eyewitness, he said.

The eyewitness to what? she said, and she thought oh no, this could come to a nasty turn now. Her heart began to thump so hard, under that foot on her blouse, that she thought, for sure, this guy could feel it there, thumping under his wandering toes, there was no doubt where that foot was now.

You're the only eyewitness to this crime, Darryl said. He smiled down at Flo. I wonder, what should I do with you?

All those people saw you too, that came and went, she said.

There was none of them that I saw with any kind of brain to remember, he said.

Then Flo found the way out that saved her, but in the long run, like I said before, how was she to know?

Ask me what I saw tonight, she said, She looked up at Darryl from the floor and willed that heart of hers to stop that dreadful pounding noise it made.

Okay, what?

I saw this guy, maybe five foot seven, a thin guy with rotten teeth and a weasel-face who came in and robbed the store and held me down on the floor with a gun, the whole time, and took all the money that came in until you came in at ten to eleven and chased him off.

I did that?

You were brave.

I was brave like a lion.

Yes you were.

Then what happened?

He ran away down the hill.

31

Like a rabbit.

You mind moving that foot please to the other side?

Like that?

That's better. That's a lot better.

How's that feel.

That feels good. The bad part was, she wasn't lying when she said that. You saved my life. You paid for smokes, you looked over the counter, you're tall, you saw me on the floor and you said to the guy, What's with the girl on the floor? And it was then that he pulled out his gun, forced you up against the rack of chips, and then he slipped out the door and ran and ran. You stayed with me. We made the call.

As she lay there, Florence could see the little man with the bad teeth running and running down Long's Hill, the lights from the passing cars, the sound of his footsteps getting smaller and smaller.

What's your name? the robber said.

Florence.

Florence, you get up now.

He reached down and gave her a hand up and dusted her off. He spent a lot of time on the blouse and on the upper parts of the jeans, where they were the dustiest.

Then, together, they put in the call to the Constabulary, and together they told the same story they'd worked on like they were old friends. Then they went out to George Street and drank up the money that Darryl had made that night. One thing led to another. They were both reckless to a fault. One day, it was too late for Florence, she'd missed three periods, maybe four, and little Queenie was on the way, unstoppable. The doctor said to her, I'm sorry Florence, there's no way, you're too far along for anything but to carry on with this little baby. That was okay with Flo. By then, she loved Darryl in her way, despite that smile he always had. We all warned her. Look at that guy, that smile of his. That I think was the worst thing we said. He could be happy, sad, busy or bored, or mean, nasty as anything, and it was the

32

always the same smile, handsome, winsome maybe to a fool, but that sick smile was forever as empty as that stupid criminal heart was of anything like kindness. Look out Florence, we said, but she never listened. She never saw it that way. It must have been how he put the sock on her chest, the knowledge he had from being older, like Flo was some kind of hostage all her life one way or another, underfoot, in the way.

You could see the writing on the wall, the late-night driving they did up and down the Number 10 Highway, the open beers that rolled on the floor, all the shady stuff that Darryl pulled, including the final trip that had something to do with crystal meth, the Winnebago that lumbered over the centre line with Darryl half-dazed, the old guy at the wheel, all that momentum they both built up when they hit. The front grill of the Winnebago went straight head-on through Darryl's rusted-up Chevrolet and it took the motor of that car, in one big jangled piece, slam-back through that smirk of his, and right through Florence too, until they all ended up in the trunk, fused and welded together by the flames that broke out, probably from the cigarette that Darryl always had to have, hanging there from his lip.

That's how Eunice inherited her baby, from her sister Flo by accident. Flo had come by earlier that day and left Queenie with her, like she'd had some kind of premonition. She was a good mother, really, when you got down to it. Here, Flo said, take Queenie a bit. Darryl and me, we're off to where there's no place for a girl.

You really can't get much better than that, when it comes to mothering.

After Butterpot

After the time she and her boyfriend Jack had open-air sex on top of Butterpot Mountain without using a condom, Tryphena Snook went home and put her feet up on the couch. She opened a magazine and fell asleep. When she woke up, she was still alone and the sun tinted the room all yellow and she thought about all the possible consequences that might ensue. Finally she said to herself, What the heck, babies run in the family, they run in all families, don't they? That's life. The Snooks were like rabbits, what could you do? She sat back and waited for her next period to come, which it always eventually did, so far anyway, like clockwork, so it wouldn't be long before the news was in, one way or the other. She couldn't blame Jack, the policeman, the man she loved, for what happened up there. The way she remembered, it was a moment of passion, the two of them together, both of them fools. She thought about it at least 600 times. She imagined an independent observer who had been there, though thank God there wasn't one, and she knew that any such independent observer would have said, with the wisdom of Solomon, that the careless young man should have had a condom on. It's his fault, not the fault of the girl. But Tryphena was not about to cast blame, it wasn't like her to do that, it was the two of them together, not just him. If she hadn't been there, lying directly underneath him as she undeniably was, like a target, there'd be no problem now at all and no concerns. Who could argue with that? Also, as her mother said, there's no use crying over spilt milk.

In the first week after Butterpot, he called her up just the same as always and they went out on dates, as usual. They went for one drive in the country, another one down to the shore. They did all the usual things and then he asked her out to a movie and they headed for the mall.

Well? he said as soon as she got in the car.

Nothing yet, she said. But I'm still not really due. Couple of days yet. Hold your horses, Sheriff.

Before the time on Butterpot, she'd called him Sheriff off and on, as a little joke, because he was a new policeman in the Constabulary. He'd liked it, then. He'd even whinnied like a horse, and slapped his hip like he was accelerating away, his hand on the reins. Now he said, Don't call me that Tryphena, I'm tired of that.

Oh? She said. Tired of it? She had the vision then of a cowboy riding off into the sunset, like they did at the end of old movies.

It makes fun of me, he said. It's belittling.

Okay, Jack, she said, Sorry, that's it then for the wild west.

He pulled into the mall and looked for a place to park. They finally found a spot but they were a long way away from the entrance. As they walked in, he said to her, Tryphie, when will we know for sure, do you think?

The evidence is not yet in, Sherlock Holmes. Bide your time, Dr Watson, she said.

He didn't laugh at that either.

Two days, Jack, that's all. Give or take a week, she said.

For some reason, after he complained about being called a Sheriff, she wanted to poke him a bit, with a stick. She didn't like the way he looked, nervous, his mind off somewhere else. It was never like this before.

After the movie was over, they went back to his place.

What'll we do? he said.

I wonder, she said.

He put on a record they both liked and then he poured a glass of red wine for Tryphena. Then he opened a beer for himself. Then they sat down on the couch, which was a bit worn-out but still serviceable, to listen to the music. Then Jack leaned over and nuzzled into her neck, and kissed her there.

Use two condoms this time please, she said.

Two? he said, that's a waste.

35

Make up for last time, she said.

She put her arms around his neck.

No, he said, one's enough. Maybe more than enough, if you're already pregnant what's the point? No condoms is fine then.

Well, she said, what kind of attitude is that? That's selfish.

Common sense, he said, that's what it is.

I'm the sacrificial lamb here, she said. I'm the one to decide about condoms.

They still had all their clothes on.

I think I'll go home and wait this out, she said.

She stood up off the couch.

Wait, he said.

It seems to me you've got your priorities all mixed up here, she said. Worry worry one moment, to hell with it all the next. What about us? she said.

She walked out into the hallway. He came up to her and pressed up against her with the whole length of his body, against the radiator.

Drive me home, she said.

He got the car keys from his coat which was hung up on the rack. He walked out into the night air with just his shirt and pants on and they got into the blue car he owned and he drove her home.

Thanks for the ride, she said when he dropped her off. She didn't say Sheriff, like she might have done before, but she did look at him real nicely and blow him a kiss. It wasn't that she didn't love him, because she did. It was just that it wasn't quite as simple as it had been before. It was like there was a tiny wedge pushed between the two of them.

Home early? Everything fine? her mother said to her.

Oh I think so, she said. I got this test tomorrow, root canals, the anatomy of nerves to the teeth.

I could never do that, said her mother. Never ever. Imagine you, Tryphie, a dental hygienist, full-blown. By the way, how's the Sheriff?

Fine, but he doesn't want to be called that any more. Belittling, he says. What do you think of that?

Got himself on a high-horse, that's what it sounds like, her mother said, They can't take a joke, watch out.

Tryphena walked up the stairs to her room. She got down all the textbooks she needed and she sat there and studied diagrams of teeth until that was all she could see. She nodded off at midnight, got up from her chair and went to the bathroom. No sign of anything there yet.

Okay Jack, she said, this is getting a bit scary.

Darling, she said.

Then she went to bed and lay in the dark, her thoughts a bit a-jumble but then she was fast asleep and dead to the world. Later on she had a dream that finally woke her up. She was at a lottery display, at one of those one-armed bandits. There were bright lights around her, like a carnival, and Jack was there, pressed up against her shoulder. There were a lot of shouts, a racket going on around them. Together they pulled on one of the arms of the money-machine, but instead of red cherries, a row of three shiny teeth came up on the screen. Molars, she shouted. Molars! They'd won! Jack jumped up and down and silver coins started to pour from the bottom of the machine all down her knees, down onto the floor in a wild cascade. She reached down to pick up a handful of those silvery coins but instead of money, all there was at her feet was a small pool of blood. There was no money there at all. What the heck? Oh it's my period, she thought when she woke up, but when she checked, there was nothing there, nothing at all. The clock said 4.30. Some dream, that one, she said to herself. Then she thought about where Jack was at that time of the morning. Halfway through the midnight shift by now, dealing with God knows what. That's where he'd be.

Actually, he'd had a pretty tame time of it so far, the way it worked out. He was doing some paperwork for a few minutes, 4.30 AM, when in came the Staff Sergeant.

There's something going on down Prescott Street, he said. Get out there Jack, check it out. Sounds domestic, weird call from some guy. They need someone, he said. Number 52.

Jack was back at the station only because he'd picked up a skinny old man wandering down by the water, wearing just a hat. That old guy made no sense at all, no surprise, so Jack had put him in the back of the squad-car and took him in. The police kept a pile of grey blankets for people like that back at the station. Mostly though, the night had been quiet. He'd driven up and down the hills in one of those cold steady rains, looking left and right like he'd been trained to, but the streets were empty of those with bad intentions.

Low psycho count so far, he said to the sergeant. Let's hope it stays that way.

Zero, said the sergeant, it's the weather, that's why. Psychos, they're all indoors. They're not as crazy as they look. Number 52, Jack. We're the only ones have to be crazy enough for this. Go for it.

The constable went out and got in his car and turned the key and all the lights came on and he set out for Prescott Street. It was all of two minutes away. When he got to the bottom of the street and looked up the hill, which was probably the steepest in a town of steep hills, there was a low mist half-way up that blocked the view. Everything looked dark and peaceful though. He drove up the hill and looked for numbers. When he hit Number 40 the mist cleared some and he could see, further up there, a light cast out onto the street from an open door. That must be it. He pulled in front of the door and he got out. He didn't put on the red flashers because that wasn't part of the drill. Not for domestics. Stay cool and calm, keep a low profile. That's the secret when you got yourself into the heart of families, whatever troubled them at 4.30 in the morning. He took his training seriously. That's how he got by.

He went up to the open door where the light was. He stopped and looked in. Even though it was raining harder now, he stayed outside. He had one of those clear plastic hat covers on, so it didn't matter about the rain. Don't rush in, he said to himself, take it easy. He'd been in these row houses lots of times, lots of times before he ever was a policeman, so he knew the layout with his eyes closed.

The first thing he saw was a man who sat on the bottom of the stairway that went up to the second floor. He couldn't see the man's face because the man had his head in his hands and his hair was all messed up and he had on one of those undershirts with no arms. Then Jack looked down the open hallway that ran back to the kitchen, all the lights on everywhere, the kitchen table neat as a pin, flowers in the centre. He thought he could hear a noise upstairs, like sobbing. He stepped through the doorway but stopped as soon as he was inside. Water ran off him onto the linoleum.

Hey what's up, Jack said in the friendly way he had. Police, he said.

The man looked up at him and stood up from the stairs. There was no smell of alcohol in the air so already there was a difference. The man had pyjamas pants on and there was something that looked like blood on the right knee.

Thank God you're here, Officer, for the love of Jesus, the man said, arrest her. She's broke the law.

He spoke louder than he had to, like he wanted to be heard throughout the whole house, through the whole neighbourhood.

Hold on, said Jack, what's the problem?

Jack didn't say, What's the problem Sir? There was something in the way the man stood there, the way he looked that Jack didn't feel like using the word Sir, even though that was part of the drill. It had to do with respect.

First she's a harlot, now she's broke the law. She's bad, bad through and through.

Who? said Jack.

He moved closer to the man.

No daughter of mine, that's for sure, the man said and he

39

started to cry. Not like he was sad for someone else. It was like blubbering.

Where is she? said Jack but then he said, Forget this.

He didn't want to wait anymore. He brushed by the man and he went up the stairs two at a time till he was on the small landing and there was a low light on in the front bedroom. He went straight there and he looked in. There was a thick heavy smell in the room of some kind. There was a plug-in night-light on the wall and that's all he could see by. On the bed in the dim light was a woman in a white nightgown lying on top of the covers, and it looked like she had her arm around the chest of a young girl. The rest of the girl was under the covers and the lady was crying though now you couldn't hear a thing from her. She was cried out, it looked like.

There she is, there she is, said the man who'd come up the stairs. He gave Jack a little push on the shoulder.

Don't touch me, Jack said. Stand back and clear the room. You, get up please ma'am. We needs to have a look here.

The lady didn't move so Jack walked over to the far side of the bed and squeezed through the small space against the wall. The girl was maybe seventeen years old, it was hard to say. Her eyes were closed but that was good. If the eyes were closed, probably that meant they were still alive. When they were dead, the eyes were wide-open, staring. This young girl had straggly dark hair on her forehead, like it was pasted there, and her face was the colour of ashes, a white-white which faded into the sheets. It was almost like she wasn't there at all. He bent down over her. He moved the woman's arm off the chest and a drop of rain fell from his hat onto the girl's cheek.

Excuse me, he said, sorry.

He could see now that she was breathing, just barely. Enough for a mouse. He pulled the covers down off her, slowly. There was nothing there from the waist down but blood and the girl didn't move at all, or even twitch when he laid her bare like that. She was unconscious. She had some kind of slip on but it didn't look like clothing anymore, drenched in the red of her own bleeding.

What in God's name is this? he said.

No-one said anything but then the man said, It's her own fault.

Jack pulled the covers back up. He moved out from the side of the bed and brushed by the man in the doorway and he went down the stairs as fast as he could. He got to the squad-car in about three seconds and he was on the radio back to the station.

Sergeant we need an ambulance. 52 Prescott.

What is it? said the Staff Sergeant.

Not your average domestic, that's for sure. I'm trying to figure it out, said Jack. Get them here fast.

He clicked the radio off and went back to the house. If anything, the rain was harder now. A few of the houses nearby had their lights on.

Take her to jail, it's okay with me, the man said.

He stood in front of the policeman in the hallway upstairs.

It's an abortion, the man said, it's a crime.

Get out of my way, you're obstructing me, said Jack. Then he added, Sir.

He was starting to feel emotional. That wasn't good but it was the hardest thing to learn in this job. He knew that.

A slut, that's what she is, the man said.

You shut up, Jack said.

Then he said to the mother, I've called the ambulance.

It was blood that caused that smell. It was the first time he'd smelled so much of it in one place. It was in the room, in the air, it poured through them all. He was sweating under the uniform even though it was cold and damp, the door still open to the outside and then he could hear the sound of the ambulance.

She's the one, she had it done, said the man.

Is this true? said Jack to the mother.

Last night, the mother said.

She sat down on the side of the bed.

Since then, she lies there like a bird, she said. Not a peep these two hours.

The ambulance pulled up outside and they came in with the stretcher. Hi Jack, they said. They all knew each other from various disasters they'd been to. They had their own small world.

Then they said, Holy Jeez, there's hardly a pulse. Here's a girl that needs blood.

They were cool, they didn't panic, they made Jack feel better. They put oxygen on her and they strapped her in and they tipped her down the stairs, with Jack out in front to lead the way.

Keep her head low, one of them said, it's better for the brain that way. Oxygen.

They rattled down the stairs but at the bottom, the father blocked the way. You can't take her to the hospital, he said, that's not for her.

Get out of the way, said Jack.

The man just stood there and he pushed Jack hard in the chest. Jack stumbled back into the ambulance man, the one at the lower end of the stretcher. He didn't fall though. He was a lot bigger than the other man.

There's got to be charges laid first, said the man. It's a crime in this country, all of this.

You're right, said Jack, so how's this? You're under arrest for obstructing a police officer.

He took the father by the front of his undershirt, turned him, and slammed him up against the wall, face-first. He'd seen it done on TV a million times and it felt good. Then he got out his handcuffs. He'd practised it and he was good at it, one or two quick moves with the wrists and it was done and he had the father out onto the street and into the back of the squad-car.

Sit there, he said.

He closed the door. Then he went back to the ambulance.

That was good, said one of the ambulance men.

Jack leaned through the back door of the ambulance and then he climbed in and stood over the girl's face and he bent down. He spoke into her ear, he said, You'll be fine. It'll all work out for you, my dear.

More water dropped from him, onto her face. She didn't feel a thing. Her matted hair still stuck on her forehead like a rag. He got out of the ambulance and stood in the street.

She'll be okay, I hope, he said to the mother. You want a ride to the hospital?

She put on a coat and she closed the front door of the house and she got into the front seat of the squad-car. She looked back at her husband through the little wire cage.

What the fuck am I doing here? he said to her.

How'd it come to this? she said, but who she was talking to wasn't clear to the constable.

That was all she said and neither of them listened anymore to the man in the back. He drove down Forest Road to the hospital and pulled in by the Emergency and he left the car running outside with the heater on, though it occurred to him not to, and he and the mother went inside. He took down all the information he needed and he left the woman there and then he drove back to the station.

Here's the guy, Prescott Street, he said to the sergeant, and he went downstairs for a coffee. He did the paperwork and he walked up and gave it to the sergeant. Then for the first time in three hours, he thought about Tryphena. She'd be getting up around now. She had some kind of exam in the morning but he knew she'd have no trouble with that.

Then the phone rang.

Jack it's me, the Staff Sergeant said, I don't know about this guy, this arrest.

How do you mean? said Jack.

The real crime here's the abortion, not this.

Trust me, you weren't there. This is the crime, said Jack.

We'll get to the other part later then?

I guess so, that's not up to me, said Jack.

No, I guess not said the Staff Sergeant. I'll back you on this one.

Okay said Jack.

Then he sat there because his shift was nearly over and he thought about Tryphena. Maybe he loved her, maybe not. He was up in the air. He didn't have a lot of experience in these things and there was no magic way to know, none at all. Why'd he ever do that up on Butterpot, anyway? That was craziness, lying there on top of her like that. Even then, when he made that mistake, when he lost his head, when he was crazy, yet it was still okay with her. Afterwards she was okay. What a girl she was. She even had the presence of mind to jump up and down, try to shake it all out. He could see her there in the sun, holding onto her pants, hopping. Did that girl on Prescott Street do that, when it happened to her? Probably not, it probably happened in the dark and she was afraid to move at all.

Was it way too early to phone her up, ask her Well? Tryphie? Any sign of anything?

Yes it was, it was still way too early. Anyway, after tonight, it felt a bit crass, all of this. He put both hands on the side of his head.

All he was worried about these days, it seemed, everywhere he went, it was all the same, blood, bleeding, girls.

ALEX LESLIE

Ghost Stories

Together we leave the truck and walk into the first forest.

Where the undergrowth is too thick, out swings his machete and branches fall like hair. I slip on roots embedded in the mud, grey and round as veins coming out of the earth. He bends and hauls me up. Western light plummets through the canopy. Radiant white columns among the old growth. This is virgin forest, he told me during the long ride out in the hot truck, which means it's never been logged. These trees have been here for as long as there have been trees here.

I didn't even giggle at the word "virgin." I want to show him that I'm worth being brought here, just us.

—Was sure it'd be here. Before the road turns. Yeah that was the right road, sure of it.

He says this, stamping ahead of me like a bear.

My pant legs are slick from walking. I strip huckleberries from a branch, cover my mouth in a smash of red pulp.

—It maybe wasn't even the right road?

He sweeps his machete into the bush to his left, steps into the door cut out by the blade, and he's gone.

—Wait here, the voice he leaves behind says.

The forest drums with steady dripping. A squirrel corkscrews up a cedar, flashing a pattern to the roof of the forest. Then it's gone too.

—Uncle Frank.

The forest takes my whole voice, gives back nothing.

He read a book about the towns that were abandoned after the mining boom and we're going to find them. All the way here in the truck from his town, he told me what we will see. Empty streets and general stores in the middle of the forest. Skulls wearing wide-brim hats. He's lived on this part of Vancouver Island all his life and he recognised all the places in the book. The big mountain with the smile-shaped rock shelf in its side. The heart-shaped hollow of chanterelles. He knows all the roads. Marked and unmarked. How far all of them go.

—Uncle Frank.

—This way.

The side of his machete glows like part of a moon, a pale green moon, the forest's own. We move faster now.

—Walk careful. We're in the middle of fucking nowhere. You fall, I'll have to carry you to the truck on my back.

—I read in science class that women have better pain tolerance.

Ferns lash my knuckles with their dripping ridged tongues.

—There's tonsa stuff I can't say around you that I could say around a boy.

—Like what?

—Can't say.

He laughs, never looks at his feet. I force myself not to look down, to walk like him, as if I've memorised the ground like a map of stones and roots. An ant watches me fall onto it. I feel its body crush on my stomach and my lips press into leaves smooth and moist as skin.

—Watch out, little girl.

His muscled arms hoop my waist and I fly far up and land on the rubber muscle of his laughter, pounding my back.

—Let me down let me down let me down.

He swings me, releases me. My feet break through bracken, into mud thick as poured concrete, push through into the water under everything.

—Come on get going.

We come out under a logging road, a deep cut across a hill's pale belly. The clear-cut around the road has shown all of the hill's guts to the sun, left them to dry and blow, except for the scrap the loggers gathered into piles he calls honeypots.

—Must be a new road. They been all up in here the last

47

month or so. Fuckers.

He points at the honeypots.

—Lookit all the wood they're goin' to burn up. Burn it all up.

A piece of metal sticks out of the ground and he kneels and scrapes the machete against its surface, as if he's shaving meat. The metal extends past his shoulder, a thin line pointing the way to the hill.

—The old railroad. Knew it was here.

—There was a railroad here?

—You think they carried out the stuff mined on their backs?

—So's the ghost town over that hill?

—First we find the old railroad, then the town.

He kneels, runs a finger over the metal, bends right down and sniffs it.

—Lot of it's gone now. This piece ain't that long.

—Did it rot?

His laughter smacks off the scraped hill.

—Metal don't rot. Shit you're dumb sometimes. Gonna snow later.

He fingers the rail. Dark and worn, like a piece of old bone. He presses gently, feeling for a beat or for a warmth.

—So?

—Shoulda put your jacket on in the truck. You get sick, you'll fuck up our day and your mom'll kill me.

—You're in shorts.

His legs are always tanned, even in winter. It's all the years walking around in the bush that does it, I think. Dirt under his skin. Dry stuff in his blood.

He walks past me, back into the forest, his machete swinging in his hand, a metronome flashing a message back to me through the trees. I am hypnotized by its swinging, stand and watch time pass, then, stunned, I run after him into the sound of water.

He never cuts more than one path. A few years ago, when he first started taking me with him on rides, I told him that using his machete in the forest was cruel. He said that if you don't cut down much, it'll all grow back in a few months, that humanoids—that's what he calls people—fuck up the bush so much with bulldozers that a few little paths don't matter.

—Don't know how anybody can sleep in a city. Humanoids should be more like deer.

Back in the truck, he covers the wheel with maps. Pencilled notes, dates of trips, where he's seen black bears and eagles, road conditions, how many logging trucks, how big their loads were. Logging trucks have right of way, always. They made these roads. When the trucks roar by, I look up out my window at their loads, teetering log pyramids.

He takes a Mountain Dew out of the cooler behind the seat. I grab one too.

—That one mine, too?

—No.

I tie the can up with my arms.

—Stop that. Jeez you're scaring me. What an ugly, scary face on a little girl.

He starts the motor and the road opens out to gold, wild grass, the ocean nodding over the trees. He slurps his Mountain Dew, lets out belches like the trombones in beginner band, jerking the steering wheel to avoid the large stones in the road. He calls the stones niggerheads, a word my dad told me I can't say. Niggerheads. Niggerheads. Niggerheads. Logger word. Island word. The logging company doesn't smooth out these roads; they're only used until all the trees in a part of the island are all gone. Then more roads are built somewhere else and the bushes and people like him fight for the old roads.

—Is your mom crazy?

Panic starts in my belly.

49

—I dunno. You mean crazy lady crazy or crazy crazy?

—Crazy crazy.

—Dunno. What do you mean.

When she's angry, I'm inside a house with no stairs. Just floors and floors. I ride down the steep hill near our house with my legs up, ankles out, pedals kaleidowhirling, and I want her to run out of the house just in time to see a car smash me in sideways.

I tilt my head back and raise my arm so the Mountain Dew falls in a long stream and babbles when it hits the pond in my mouth.

—Stop that. You know how much this truck cost?

—How much?

—Less than your spinal operation if you spill that.

I stick my nose into the can and smell the Mountain Dew because he smelled the piece of railroad. Tin, lemon dish soap. He does that kind of thing. Tastes the water on leaves. Licks his finger and sticks it up to feel the wind. Kicks bear turds open.

Berries. We're near where they're eating these days. This way instead then.

—I seen your mom screamin at your dad. I never yelled at Barb that bad and I met her when I was sixteen.

I stare at him, nervous. How much did he see?

—So? Maybe you guys're just boring.

—Bein borin's not bein not crazy.

—You've lived here all your life. That's pretty boring.

He jerks the wheel to the side, pushes down on the gas. I see a rocky slope looming, the bottom piece of the sky fading into a fan of trees. I scream.

Grinning, he pulls the truck back onto the road and drives on, the same as before, rumble steady, bumping into clouds, frozen light coming off the ocean. Nothing all the way to Japan, he told me once.

—Boring's actin like you're in the fuckin circus.

He doesn't say this until a few minutes later.

I get up on my knees on the seat, hold my can of Mountain Dew out the window and pour it out. He bellows. I take his can of Mountain Dew from the padded cup holder and stick the top half of my body out the window. He's yelling.

—You're crazy like your mom. Get back in the fucking truck.

I smile back at him. My ears torn open by wind. I am crazy like her. Doing this for no reason, loving how much he hates it.

When my parents scream at each other in the kitchen, my mom always ends up forcing my dad out onto the deck, slamming the glass sliding door shut to keep him out in the cold. Once I walked in for a glass of milk during one of their fights and saw my dad on the porch, beating his fists on the glass. He was yelling but all I could hear was one word, again and again.

—In. In. In.

She stood on the warm side of the glass, drinking a cup of tea. The cup floated in the white light coming through the glass, just under his red face, steaming.

The rushing air lifts the stream of Mountain Dew, bends it like a string of yellow-green cheap necklace pearls. I watch it waver behind us, then splash into the truck's side, each drop exploding one by one, breaking like frail glass, draining off like light.

There's something wrong with her but I don't know what.

—Get back in here. Just get back in here. In the truck. Come on. Okay, now.

When we stop, he skids down the bank to a stream and comes back with a soaked rag, wipes the Mountain Dew off, moving the rag in circles so it won't leave streaks.

—Why'd you do that, crazy girl? Go wash out the rag.

I cross my arms so he puts the rag on my shoulder and walks away.

When I get back from the stream, he holds up each arm of

my jacket as I slip into it.

—See? I'm a gentleman.

—You look like a logger.

I say it because it's the worst insult I can think of.

He shrugs. His shoulders roll like water, drop hard.

—I been a logger for a while when I was round nineteen.

—Lying.

—Went into jobs on a tiny plane that jumped around and every guy threw up.

—Every guy? Yeah right.

—The floor of that plane was a lake of barf.

—Sick.

—That's all they got in China. So polluted they got lakes full up with barf.

—Lying.

—I seen it on TV last week. That's what's gonna be here too.

—Like when?

—Couple hundred years.

—So what then?

I worry all of a sudden that he's forgotten why we came.

—Ghost town!

—Don't crap yourself. I got the map here. You think it's North or South?

—I dunno.

—They said you was smart.

—Were smart not was smart. Too bad you didn't finish high school.

—North or South?

He puts his arms around his round junk-food stomach, the only part of him that isn't muscle.

—North.

Shake his head, blue eyes faking mournful.

—Wrong. Dead North from this point, little girl. Let's go.

He takes the machete from behind his seat, zips up his

windbreaker and drops cans of mountain dew, shrink-wrapped pepperoni, Oh Henry bars, half a loaf of bread, his maps and the ghost town book into his backpack. He thinks, then drops in his flashlight.

We walk into the second forest.

This forest is different from the first. No rain. I miss the sound of water, the tick-tock of a watery clock buried in the mulch. The light here thinks and shifts, pale browns and greys, the colours of the birds who dance around his glass feeders on his porch back in town, where he melts Kraft cheese onto steaks on the barbecue and shoots his BB gun at the cats who stare from the leaning fences, their slanted eyes shimmering, starving. He's a soldier for the island birds. The birds that were brought in from England a hundred years ago that he says steal from the island birds, he leaves for the cats.

—You said it'd be close.

—What you gonna do? Turn back?

I'm going to turn back. I'm going to find the truck and figure out how to drive it back to the town where my mom and dad are drinking ginger ale and arguing with my relatives about the price of gas and whether it's safer to live in a city where there're more police or in small towns where, my grandmother says, there is a cocaine bust every day. She hears it all happening on her police scanner that she keeps turned on all day in her kitchen. I'm going to drive them all back to the city on the mainland.

I track the last scrap of his black bear back between the branches.

—Coming or what?

This forest is a dry box I could sit down in, gather the walls around me, make a hood from the soft brown leaves and all the needles like matches and eyelashes. I will forget about the black, wet rainforest we were in an hour ago. I'll build a fort and roast pinecones and eat the sweet feet of mice trapped inside that I've heard about in campfire stories all my life, before they cut down every last tree, every last piece of this place, like he says they will. This whole island will be a bare rock in the ocean off Vancouver. The ferries will charge tourists to come here and climb up its dry sides, read plaques bolted to the rocks about living things that used to be here, look at satellite photos of rainforest canopies, black skies stencilled with life, the faces of the countries of men that immigrated to slice them down, our coast written into the context of the dinosaurs, all the old, dead things made magic by doom. That's what he says.

—How come you brought your machete this time if you don't need it here.

We walk quickly over the dry, crackling ground. Instead of sweating, sharp ferns there's a carpet of branches, rows and rows of white flowers.

—Machete's not only for bush. No other humanoids out here you're gonna see. Lots that could happen.

He stops, puts up one hand, turns to face me.

—You hear that?

I stop.

I hear wind like decks of cards being shuffled by invisible players crouching in the bushes and, under everything, a hum. One bird. Two birds. Four?

—I don't hear anything.

—Yeah you do. You hear the forest. And you think the forest gives a shit about you?

He doesn't say it like a challenge, just like it's true.

—No. Yeah. Yeah, maybe it does. Yeah, it does. No. Does it?

—Yeah it does.

—So. Then why'd you bring the machete then?

—Makes me feel more safe.

—Carrying a knife would make me feel more scared.

—That's cause you don't know how to use a knife.
—So show me then.

So he does. The handle heavy in my hand. The blade shows my whole face, my chin sliced off at the light-slicked edge, my eyes sliding away. My arm sinks under its weight when I don't concentrate on it, supporting its heavy threat.

—You gotta move it fast and know where you're aiming. Never cut toward yourself. Always aim away. You could cut your leg off like that, little girl. Wouldn't be the only leg here, though.

We'll see more. He promises me a graveyard.

He's the one who teaches me these things, every time my parents drive up here. How to stop a boy from breathing with my two thumbs, their joints glued together like a wishbone's V. How to skin and whittle a branch so it flies and breaks skin. How to build a fire on a beach. Find the dry wood between the big beach logs. The ocean spits up those logs like toothpicks. Your body is floss.

Back in Vancouver, I keep these lessons for myself. The cherry blossom trees that foam up pink around the school hold secret weapons. Everybody in my city family looks down on him—his grammar, his gym shorts worn to dinner, his swearing, the pattern of his sweat around his T-shirt collar like a tattoo.

—What'd you mean asking me is my mom crazy?

I'm surprised how angry I sound, but if I take it back, he won't answer.

—She's not all there.

He keeps walking, shrugs, like it's just obvious.

My legs hurt but I won't say so. He swings his camera now instead of his knife. The lens cap hangs loose and the camera's glass eye flashes like a pool of black oil at his hip. It's late afternoon, light coming down thicker through the branches, stamping the ground with spines and teeth, as if skeletons are slung in the canopy, throwing down sharp shadows, and we are wandering the open spaces between their bones.

—Loggers'll trash the town when they get to it. Clearcutting'll get there this summer. They cut down more every summer. Want to get some good shots for the album.

He has a closet full of photos of the trips he's gone on around this part of the island since he was a teenager.

—What do you mean my mom's not all there?

He stops and takes the ghost town book out of his bag, stands in the shadow of a huge tree and flips through the pages.

—Yup, we're almost there.

His baseball cap is pulled low over his eyes, his shoulders thick and blocky as chunks of fireplace rock.

—Just tell me.

I know he's the only one who'll tell me the truth. Everyone else lies to my face about my mom. I know it. They say it's stress. She's under a lot of stress right now. Or, work takes a lot out of her. Or, she needs more time for herself. I know that they are all lying. Other people's anger isn't like hers, and I know it. I know that one day she will get angry and she will be gone. I spend a lot of time imagining it happening in different ways. She'll explode, a red cartoon bomb. She'll fade piece by piece like the people in Back To The Future, sucked away, cheeks then feet then hair, clutching her chest for air, breathing me in. Or nothing will happen. She'll just disappear.

—Not all there. Not all there.

He looks down at me.

—She don't look me in the eye. Ever seen her get really mad? She don't know how to stop. I don't know, kid. Not all there. Means something's missing. Don't know what. Just not there.

I look at him, my voice floating away from my body.

—Was it there before?

The forest's dark fills in all the lines in his face. I can't tell what he's thinking. I can never tell what he's thinking. He shrugs, shadows like green pillows on his shoulders.

—Don't matter, does it. Now that it's gone, eh?

He carries me on his back when I can't walk anymore. Hook my arms around him, float on his body like deep water with its own gentle currents.

—You can sleep if you want.

—But then I'd let go and fall.

His Adam's apple buzzes under my linked fingers like a drowsy bee cupped there.

—If you fall asleep hanging on really tight, your hands'll stay that way. Gotta hold on tight.

He rocks me a bit.

—Here we are little girl. Here's your ghost town.

I pull my tired eyes open and see lines in the night between his neck and shoulder.

—Look this was the road they made through it.

His flashlight's on, snagging on roots, leaves jumping out like wallpaper rockets, and the yellow tube of light wanders slow over grassy spaces between the walls of trees, like one eye we're both seeing through.

—You seeing it? You awake?

He walks faster down the middle of the road. He breathes fast, excited.

The flashlight chooses for us. The front of a white church worked over by bugs, tides of dried needles and leaves lining the old road as if the ocean washed them here, a door standing without its walls, darkness surrounding both sides completely, the carcass of some animal at its stoop, as if the animal was struck dead trying to go through that door to what was on the other side.

—Holy shit lookit that.

I don't, whatever it is he's found now. I hide from the ghost town behind his neck. I feel the shapes of the dead

57

houses around us as we walk slowly down the main street.

He puts me down on an ancient tree's arched root, tall as a bench, and we drink Mountain Dew and chew pepperoni and white bread. He puts an arm around me and pulls me against him until I stop shaking, shivering.

Tomorrow I will drive back to the city with my parents. The ferry ride to the mainland will feel, like it always does, like a crossing between worlds. My mom will cry in the ferry line-up, scream at the apologetic BC Ferries guy in his navy shirt, her voice rising like shrill wind. I will want her to disappear, beg for her to disappear.

—Pretty neat, eh? Glad we came. Too dark for photos.

He'll come back here, again and again, until the logging company carves its own road through this forest. Then he'll come and take photos of the clear-cut when they're finished, the small white stumps he always says look like grave markers.

—Good you saw this, little girl. It'll all be gone, soon enough.

Swimmers

He falls asleep on a beach in the city's elbow and night blows newspapers over him. In the morning rain has soaked yesterday's newsprint across his forehead, yesterday's news. Dawn is happening. First light on water, first ink.

Sidewalk unrolling there to stumble up, away from the Pacific. Back up the street past all last night's doors. Kids across the street, parallel lines pointing the way to school, jackets in every primary colour, shouting morning.

Just dance. Club darkness muggy with liquor breath, ice cubes snapped between teeth and under rhythmed feet, bare shoulders like lit fish teeming the crowd's surface. Faces press into the glass of each other. Who are you? Come near me. Get away. He dances like a third-grader, like a sexbot, like a snake charming another snake. Jump up, flap arms, shimmy down and move your butt, every slut since Chaucer knows that move.

Dark early-morning/mid-night. Rain hurtles down gutters toward the ocean. He breathes himself out into the chill air, a clove-scented cloud following the street to the water. This is where he comes after everything every day is done.

The first time she sees him. Shoulders like a tall riverhunting bird, eyes trapping fish thoughts. Black hair swinging low. His laugh, making a crack in the sounds of traffic. He lies on the curb laughing, a body like wires thrown down on the road by a windstorm, electricity startling his arms and legs, hurling back the bodies of others.

She sees him most nights in the places they both go.

On the balcony above the crowd, looking down at the bodies swinging together, they rest and drink and watch the dancing ocean, heads and arms tossed into light.

—Why are they all here?

—Fashion, fun, drinking, sex, nothing.

They become a familiar creature. This strange space that will keep them together.

This season sidewalks make glistening land-bridges between seas of yards and streets, cement and metal and plastic signs, and everybody in the city waits for sunlight, waits to surface.

Every night, they meet at the same corner. They dive into a dancing crowd again, again, but each wave of music pushes them back to where they began. She does not think of her classes that feel like bloodletting, the dimming eyes of her daylight friends. Outside, dark-veined rain lifts up the city's lights.

Take my hand, turn me round. Nightworld, forest of glinting dull-eyed buildings, this nightwood. They spill out onto another street. The ocean glowing at the endpoint of the gutter's slope, the moon's turned bright stone.

They don't talk to each other about their lovers. She goes to bed with a girl in one of her classes. It feels like the swell around a smoothed-out knot on driftwood, a strong turn of bone between two of her fingers and smoothness shouldn't be mistaken for softness. Her body something long and turning between her palms, something loose, rope-like. She holds her hard, a surprised face freezing in the air, like that, between reliefs. It is something.

He goes to the park beside the ocean. Men slide among the quiet trees. Their chests reflect light, the smoothness of the urban lake in the distance, dark mirror littered with crisp curling leaves.

He guides her eye with one extended finger.

—All the people in my world are crazy, see?

Laughing, face stretched and turning through rye-rinsed glass.

—The guy at the all-night gourmet french-fries place, the

one with the cute/robot voice, he's crazy, see? This is what it's like when you live at night.

He has a job during the day but she doesn't know what and she doesn't ask. Her days of classes, students in rows faces turned to the blank light. When she mentions class his face goes blank with disinterest or lack of recognition. She is surprised to discover how simple it is to slice off nights from days, light from dark. How easy to double up on silent living, hold one hand beside the other without touching.

—Shit what was that sound?

A wave of crashing on the pavement, a piece torn off the sky.

—A car just went through the window of that store. Right through that huge window.

A busy street but pedestrians sidestep, keep moving, their voices and the horns of other cars rising in chorus. The driver stumbles off unharmed with his phone pressed into his ear, a gash like a red feather pressed to his forehead.

She taken a picture of her dancing partner posing glum-faced with the fresh wreck. Metal dug out and twisted. In the image stored in her phone: an astronaut posing with his stranded craft, street moonscape cratered with starlight, streetlight. This is her only evidence, she thinks.

A man sprints down from the apartment above the store and a shy cornered fire is smothered as instantly as it started.

He points at the crowd coming out of the Blenz at midnight. Students slope down the oilslick street. Jeans like denim leggings. Earmuff headphones. Briefcases moulded around laptops. Shoulderbagsipodsleathertinybuttonsplansplansplans.

—Robots.

—What makes a person not a robot?

—That line between capacity and ability.

Just dance. How much can happen in what amount of time?

How they fall into the folds, surf the edges for months, not wondering.

Dancers flee from heavy bass like birds sensing a thunderstorm. Monsoon season in Vancouver. Busses are hired boats, nosing flooded corners and river-bends posted with newspaper boxes, moving rows of picture windows of faces soaked with the future months of water, dark with the knowledge of their collective slow drowning.

Before, she had a theory she doesn't believe in anymore. All-encompassing adolescent invention. Hit her in high school physics class. Looked up to the blackboard on a day late in winter, glassy classmate faces stained opal, and saw it there, a phrase from the clouds: Particles of energy exist on different levels and their travel between is untraceable. The same goes for people, she thought.

Thinking a round trap. Minds are winding or they are still, brain quiet as burping frogs in a wet ditch. What is between this dug-up turning and women with taped-on smiles riding all the busses splashing up water-wings from the gutters? She saw it then—no belief in epiphanies, just in fossil selves coming up under the skin, the blank levels people walk on, rows and rows and rows.

Now, she stares into the open darknesses between buildings, bodies, days. She could be pulled into those spaces, a body disappearing.

—Get that heart off your sleeve. Be more scary-lady, more regal-trashy, more you.

—Diana Ross, Jane Fonda with caterpillar drag queen eyebrows.

—Celine Dion as a crypt keeper, waltzing with a mannequin.

—Would you stop it with the references?

—I think I need a lobotomy while I sculpt dead air.

Just dance. Impulse over awkwardness. Fascination. What will the body do without thought? Pull in liquor like spacemen drinking nozzle-mouthed air, glass-faced, music lifting bodies from this blind floor. Underworld trappings. Nothing more cliché so turn off all the lights.

—I am tired of the helplessness of desire of everyone around me.

—Don't pigeonhole people.

—People. Pigeons in their holes.

They dive into the ocean at the foot of the street. He sees her body moving away from his, a radiant thick fish. Through strong water, she is a dancer under black light. She sees him swept, close and far. She slips under. He floats nearby, his skin faded blue and his eyes flashing ciphers, and he raises his arms and gyrates, his limbs slowed by the weight of water. She looks upward. Here, seen from underwater, the city hangs from its concrete roots. Reflections of buildings dangle from the surface, windowed spears, entering her eyes as she swims upward toward the air of the world. It is raining and the raindrops wash the salt from her eyes, burns the world new.

Windows of late-night workers, dull white squares in the sky, spreadsheet star-chart. The dark rooms they move through, music coming out of the bouncing floor, the floor moving like a chest, the heart inside it a drum under the floorboards, old hard beat. Music pushes up through her muscles, works them until they hurt and pulse with waterfisted rhythm.

He shouts over the sound.

—When I'm too old to come to these places, I'll get married. Ice sculptures, martinis and silver body paint.

They walk into the rain like seals underwater, water

parting around their bodies, preordained paths in the thick airborne wet of this city.

She sweeps a hand at his dark-eyed bravado.

—No, you'll marry a boy with a dog and gym shorts on Sundays. All of Canada will join you at the lake.

She finds him outside a club, crying against a brick wall about an older lover who said, I only wanted to be good with you, then disappeared into the dancing bodies, the lights and small glasses flashing. Who is he? She asks him. How long was he with the lover? He shakes his head, shrugs, because there are relationships that come and go, fade and appear but are always there, are untraceable in they paths they work. She does not know him at all, she knows.

—People will say anything to get to you.

—Anything if that's what they want: you.

—Can't give yourself if you don't.

Mornings. Lawnmowers hunt at her basement suite windows, crawl up like metal-headed mice. Thrum of waking eyelids. Just waiting for night again, gnawing for darkness, headaches the colour of sunlight, stretching the curtains to keep the brightness out. Spring starts. Everywhere sunlight, a common insult, shameless sparkle. But still the rain. He sings: You come and go, you come and go. Mantra of the undecided.

—I can't do this anymore.

No beginning for this. Falls like a black bird shot out of the windowed sky.

—What do you mean?

—I'll stop thinking and will be ordinary.

—I don't know. I'm the same.

She always knew he was held together by the tinsel that glitters at the corners of his eyes when excited or breaking. People with sturdy reassurance scrape her deep as the thickness of a fingernail.

She staggers into lightfooted ground. She watches the club's searchlights sweep his chameleon skin, colours flashing through smoke like a weather system working out its hurricane core.

The top half of the province is burning, the bottom half is sliding into the sea, the part above that is melting. This is always the way the weather ends, they say it in all three newspapers.

He watches her slide between beats thrown off the ends of the DJ's fingers. She is his guest from the daylight hours, fallen through the trapdoor. Where did she come from and when will she leave? They gather shooters on the bar near their dancing, amber, honey-brown, orange, a collection of fireflies trapped under glass.

She waits for him on their corner, in all the usual places. She hasn't seen him for six nights, a width of wordless nights.
No rain tonight.
Fog ghosts rub their white bellies on the black streets.

She watches the dancers, silent traffickers of shadow and light, lovers without lovers. She looks for him down by the ocean.
The Pacific moves out there, a separate black planet. Sound of a broom sweeping the sky clean of its hard sharp stars. Top layer of water moving on and off, dark eyelid for the shining day of water.
He told her once that instead of paying for taxis some early-mornings after dancing he fell asleep in the sand, stretched against a log, invisible from the street above. Once

a newspaper blew over him and dew soaked it against his skin, printing the cheap ink onto his cheek, a direct transfer tattoo. He told her how he crouched in the surf and washed off yesterday's headlines, walked to his job damp, head spinning with fading liquor and the waves that pounded on last night's washed-up bed.

She walks slowly among the logs, calling his name, morning birds chirping angrily at the human racket.

Spinning in the darkness of static/rain. The sparks from blown-out speakers hit wet skin like fireflies and stars and bodies swim together. Her limbs move slowly underwater. She does not know what it is for anymore, listening to her thoughts like the heartbeats of other people.

It is exhausting to be a chameleon, it's a headache to wake blue and sleep green, to eat yesterday's words and to not know the next day's. She does not know what that will be, what she is now.

Now she knows how to do tricks with her skin. This is what she learned from him. An allergy to one temperature of air, a witness protection program for the other person living inside. Where did he come from and where did he go?

That brightness from before what was that. Darkness now. Moods, cold water tickling long fingers down, looking for something in weather.

When we dovetail darkness like this we can't get away. Why he plunged when she did. Made a space in her, a small cave in the corner of her foot, too out-of-the-way to be worn down by leaving.

She climbs the stairs through darkness to the balcony above the dance floor and watches through her glass, looking for him. The bodies below, vertical, hands swinging, dogs swimming through rough water.

She sees him once in daylight:

Holding a pocket thesaurus open in one palm, flipping the waxy pages, fingers flickering like a waterwheel. She always thought it was a joke, what he said about himself: Barstar to bookstore. The fluorescent lights, off-white linoleum, neat dark lettering, worlds packed in volumes placed in rows and rows around him. His face resting, eyebrows up, arch dandy put-on. His patchwork jacket and dark-rinse jeans. His cheeks the pale tenderness of a fish's soft underbelly. Inked shadows under his eyes. A creature pulled from the bottom of a shining tank and left on carpet. She watches him, fingers skimming spines of bestsellers gold and cerulean thriller blue, and knows that she is saying goodbye. She is saying goodbye to her friend.

He strides toward an exit, the PA system barking news of the summer's coming bargains. The spinning rack of bestsellers she hides behind, gold and purple covers, metal branches, a wild indoor tree, but any shelter is good enough.

Leave it like oil on a wet road. All the people passing through this life will smear and press in the old bloodlet stuff, it will be a stain on her skin she can only see when she traces its edges with her fingers. Don't dare to try, she tells herself, don't make it spread and shimmer. There is nothing after blacklung bitterness, the only thing is what to do after and after. Capture a daylight lover. Things quickly change away from here.

Morning streets and rain has washed all the city's ink away.

Preservation

They would kill us if they knew what we do here, in the turtle pit. Her hands clench behind my neck like a second bundle of optic nerves, giving my eyes the strength to withstand the intense glare of this place—black rock walls, washed-out sky. Above the turtle pit, the fields sweep out for gold miles all the way to the town where everyone lives. We crawl under the truck. Its shadow is the only escape from the heat. Underneath, it smells of oil, dust and our sweat. All the fossils in the turtle pit lie in heaps around us. The sharp mouths of rocks bruise us as we roll and our cries echo back for millions of years.

Once, after we make love, she reaches across my body and takes a trilobite from beside my shoulder. She holds it over us—a small prehistoric creature, its back patterned like a brain. I run my finger along the black contours of its form, then around the lines of her body. We scramble into the hot light and pull our clothes over our bodies. I jump into my jeans. She buttons up the long skirt that she has to wear, even in summer. She slides the trilobite into my pocket where it bulges beside my wallet.

"Wait, wait," I say and rummage in the truck for my camera.

"No, no," she protests, smiling, then afraid.

"Just stand there."

This is the image of her that I will keep. Arms akimbo, her wild smile, like a kid posing with Mickey Mouse at Disney Land, one of the turtles at her side. The black shape absorbs all light, bends all space toward it. Then, a long sequence of her standing at mock attention, hands linked around her slim stomach. As I click the shutter again, again, she stares solemnly into the camera's small eye, the fossilised turtle resting at her side. Then she bends and kisses its blunt black top, hard, falls to her knees with her arms around it. My

68

laughter bounces and shines off the rock walls.

My dad and my stepmom Anne named it the turtle pit. The pit was dug out by a logging company to get rock to grind up for roads, then abandoned. The walls are loaded with fossils—once, it must have been a riverbed or cove, protected and fertile. My dad found the turtle pit on the way back from a camping trip. He took Anne, an amateur fossil nut, then me. We stared at the turtles coming out of the earth like tumours or diamonds. I ran my fingers over them, feeling something garish and magical in me.

A few months later, they drove out there in the truck of a friend who works in construction and used his equipment to lift two of the turtles into the back of the truck. They set one turtle down on either side of the door to our house. Door ornaments, or prehistoric sentinels. A real hoot, they said. Walking between them for the first time, I couldn't help but feel judged by the ages. The week before, I had met her.

It was my idea for us to start going to the turtle pit. It was just two hours out of town and at the end of its own abandoned road. In the back of my mind, I was reassured that a place made of rock couldn't keep a record. All soft surfaces could betray us with the marks of our bodies.

Every afternoon after we made love for those first few weeks in her house, we stood in the laundry-room while the washing machine churned the sheet clean. It was our ritual. Hip against tilted hip; breast against breast; the white metal edge of the machine against her back or mine. The basement room barely lit by the sun that worked its way through the ground-level window. We listened for her father's footsteps above us. Once, I had to scramble out the window and crawl along the side of the house to walk the mile to where I had parked my truck.

It was only a matter of time before someone walked into the empty house when her bedroom was live with the sounds of us.

"It'll be safe there," I told her. I drove her past our house quickly, once, and she craned her neck to see the turtles by the door. My stepmom Anne waved at my truck from the front window.

We've been coming here ever since, for months now, to the turtle pit. One narrow road leads down into it. The tire marks from my truck wrinkle the dust. After every visit, I walk up and down, checking for others, then kneel and wipe ours away.

All the houses on our side of town are full of stuff found on the beaches—foam buoys the weight of volcanic rock, smoothed glass, and shells printed with galaxies. Glass floats, beautiful as bathyspheres, picked from kelp beds. Cans of pop that drifted, unopened, all the way from China. Someday a researcher will go around and collect all this stuff, put it together, and write a true report about everyone who lives here.

An archaeologist. That's what I'm going to be. I can dig through and pull out what matters, I tell her. I have a way with layers. She laughs, pulls the back of her hand across my cheek, then holds it around my breast. "Sure you are," she says. The piping of the truck's belly shines above her like the dark network of a body. She hates making love in front of the turtles. "I feel like they're watching us," she whispers.

In her part of town, decorations harvested from beaches are absent from porches and mantels. Wooden houses like cabins stand side by side, cut from the same tube of frozen cinnamon-coloured cookie dough. We met at the Hallowe'en dance at the skating rink—the only chance for kids from the high school and the Traditional school, the thumper school, to meet. The ice had been melted off for repairs, revealing a dance floor of concrete that was unbelievably smooth. She stood with the girls from the thumper school. They looked like the back-up singers for a kitschy German band. They bent down and held their noses above the skin of the punch, suspecting liquor.

I watched her walk onto the dance floor. Her movements to the song were all off. Anyone could tell that she had never danced before. Her legs bowed and swayed under her long skirt. I began to measure time by the movements of her body, not the beats in the music. People stood in a circle around her. The thumper kids backed up. She danced until a tall boy about my age strode forward and stilled her with a finger on her elbow. Oh God, I thought. Not this. Not her.

I can smell my dad from the front door. He sits in the underwater light of the living-room, feet up, his fingers around his bottle like a cradle of dirty white rope.

"What're you doin' now?" he says. I hear it wrong, as, "What're you gonna do?" because it's all I think about— when I will leave town, and how I can take her with me. I can't stay around here wearing jeans and driving a truck after graduation. No woman can do that, here.

"I'm going to be an archaeologist," I say.

"Sure you are," he says, his eyes fixed on Dr. Phil. "Ark-ee-oil-oe-jist. Last job I did was cleaning out someone's basement. The pipes were broke. Not the water pipes. The shit pipes. That's a bad job to have. Shovelling out a basement of half-frozen shit. I pretended it was cookie dough." He drains the rest of his beer. "Isn't that what an ark-ee-oil-oe-jist does, though? Digs through everybody else's shit."

I have been reading about fossils in the magazine Anne subscribes to. Fossil comes from the Latin fossus, meaning "having been dug up." A living fossil is an informal term—a living species that's a lot like a species that is now living. A trace fossil is activity left in the rock. A fossil isn't something that worked to get that way. All it takes is the right place, minerals, compression, and then millions and millions of years. Also, I spent part of the summer reading On the Origin of Species by Means of Natural Selection, or the Preservation of Favoured Races in the Struggle for Life by

Charles Darwin.

I see myself in a basement, shovelling shit out a window.

"What're you just standing there for?" I have discovered recently that he hates it when I look at him.

"You're a living fossil," I say.

He gets up, steps toward me.

"What the fuck did you just say?"

I drive the truck as fast as I can across the town to her house. People on the sidewalk stop and look at my truck. I stop pounding on her door when a man opens it. I recognize him from her stories.

"Can I help you?" he says.

I take a step back. My ears are stuffed with tiny violins. Trees bristle with the static of wings—birds on their way out.

"Is she here?"

"Is who here?"

I say her name.

"Yes, she's here. Can I tell her who's looking for her?"

He looks past my shoulder at the truck.

"Where do you live?" he says. "How do you know her?"

She slides up, beside his elbow. "What's going on?"

"Do you know this girl?" her father asks her.

He angles his logger's body toward hers. More than half the men in town are loggers and the other half work in the mill. On windy days, the mill blankets the town with a smell exactly like rotten eggs burning in an old cast-iron pan.

"No," she says. "I don't know her."

"Sorry," he says. "It seems you have the wrong house."

The next afternoon, she folds socks in the laundry-room and pretends not to hear my fingernails, palms, then knuckles against the glass. She opens the window an inch.

"Are you crazy? The neighbours will hear."

"Let me in."

"I can't."

72

"Why not?" My clothes are filthy from sleeping in the truck last night.

"My father heard about the dance."

"Does he know about us?" She doesn't answer, holds her arm against the window so I can't open it any further. "What did you tell him?"

"He saw how you were looking at me. But he already knew."

"How?"

"Please leave. The neighbours will hear."

"How?"

"Last year. They wanted me to leave. He told them it wouldn't happen again."

"You told me I was the first."

"Was I yours?"

My knees are numb from kneeling and fear.

"Yes." I put my fingers through the small opening in the window. Her skin feels like stone. "Please let me in."

"I'll be cast out," she says.

I push the window the rest of the way open.

"Hell."

I climb onto the laundry machine and then down onto the floor.

"Close the window," she says. "The neighbours will hear."

I close the window. It is as if all of the muscles in her body give up and stop when I touch her. She lets me lie her back on the pile of laundry to be washed. His laundry. All the smells of this place rise around our bodies. Wood shavings, sweat. I grasp fat handfuls of her skirt, her everyday uniform.

During those hours in the pit as we made love under the truck, she often raged against this skirt, against the husband her father has chosen. I saw him at the dance. He was the one who led her out of the cheering circle on the floor. He was lean and caramel-coloured as an adolescent deer. I am humiliated that he is the one who will have her. Her hands clench together behind my neck. There is a permanent bruise where

73

her thumbs dig in. When that dark imprint fades, I will have lost her from my body.

I fall again and again into her and we are back in the turtle pit, protected by dark walls. I fall again and we sink farther, into the rock, and all the way down. Her hair lies across the floor like a vein of brilliant ore in the linoleum.

"I can't leave. This is my home," she says.

"What does that mean?"

She looks at me closely, as if she pities me.

"It means that this is where I'll stay until I die. It means that this is where I want to be buried."

It is raining when I climb onto the surface of the earth. I drag my legs out of the window behind me like thick, wet roots. A smear of white paint on dark glass—a face watches me through another basement window.

The sun makes the black pit into an oven. I carry armfuls of rock to the middle of the pit and pull them apart. I sit and study the imprints inside, preserved there like an ancient form of plate photography. A pit of fossils is a good place to be desperate for messages. I stare at the insides of rocks until my eyes sting and run. A large chunk falls into two parts in my hands. Inside, a network of marks like light scratches on a blackboard, too small and faint to identify. Were they tiny worms, or the last traces of something bigger that wasn't preserved? I search for a pattern until I realize that they were still in motion when this happened to them. I open more rocks. A fern's tip, the torso of a prehistoric insect. Her curved neck, the hourglass of her body.

The truck coming sounds like an avalanche in the distance. I watch the four men come down the steep road. When I see what her father holds in his hand, I stand. I hold my fossils up like weapons.

The first blow brings blindness. The sky lunges upward and darkness crumbles off the world like a wall of rock. My body falls again and again. Every time I fall, I open my eyes and see the turtles, watching this. They tell me the story of when it happened to them—how the cloud of dust came and covered their earth in a day, put their bodies far under the layers of the earth. The enormous green ocean they swam through, the fish and creatures that were their world, patterns of leaves, patterns of tide, the banks where they mated under the moon that stayed safe from the fire. It happened without reason. There was no warning except for a change of temperature in the air. It happened to us and now it is happening to you, they tell me. What you are, we once were.

JEFF PARK

Back to Disney

We drive in the dark of winter. The headlights of the Bronco illuminate a narrow path that we follow. Snow kicks up behind us.

"Don't worry about it Lindsay. Okay? Listen, they read the meter once, twice a year. Simple. Pay the bill and let it go."

"What about spikes, Jerry?" I ask.

"You paranoid or what? You keep it constant, no major changes, therefore no surges. Simple. This used to be a dairy barn. High power usage. We didn't change a thing, right?" Jerry looks over at Dave and shakes this head. "What can you do? The guy's worse than my mother. Listen, Lindsay I tracked all the bills for months. There are no surges, believe me. Those fucking cows drained a lot of power. Nothing will show up, trust me."

Jerry turns the Bronco into a farm lane framed on both sides by trees. We drive into the farmyard past a small white house and stop beside the barn. The wind blows across an empty white field. The snow rises in ridges to the tops of the fence posts. A yellow flood light on a steel pole forms a halo of light in the frosted air. We wait for a few minutes listening to the metallic clanking of the engine cooling. The wind whistles at my ear through a thin crack at the top of the side window.

Finally Jerry says, "Listen, drop it. Don't worry. I'll look after everything. Okay?"

"Fine," I say.

"Your uncle home?" asks Dave.

"No. Wednesday night he's in town."

"You ever worry about him?" I ask.

"Why should I? I give him a break on rent. He doesn't ask questions."

"You own this land?"

"You on the other hand seem to like questions."

"Just curious," I say.

"I know," says Jerry.

Jerry opens the truck door, shifts his weight to get out and turns to Dave. "We won't be long. Keep watch."

Jerry and I get out of the Bronco. The large hinged front doors of the barn are sealed. We walk through the snow to the side door. Jerry leans over and puts his gloved hand on the shoulder of my parka. I feel the weight and pressure of his hand. "I just want you to know I'm impressed. You've done a great job. The design is perfect." He nods his head and opens the side door. "Welcome to Disneyland," he says.

We step through heavy green plastic curtains. The contrast is startling. Inside the building the 500 plants under the long rows of grow lighting create a near jungle humidity. A steamy warmth rises to the wooden rafters of the sloped ceiling ten to fourteen feet above us. The 400-watt halides with round, green reflectors are suspended from the rafters. Tiny sprinkler heads hang from black plastic water pipe. Thin sprays of water mist onto the tiny plants in the eight-inch plastic pots. Plastic tubing leads to each pot. The plants are in two long metal troughs running the length of the building. Jerry leads me down the centre aisle of the plants. It feels a little like being in a church, walking between pews in silence. There is a green tinge to the light. The humidity is almost solid.

"It's beautiful," I say.

"You did fine work on the design. We've already moved most of the plants from the blooming-room. Your system is incredible," Jerry says.

"I know I designed the set up and everything, but to see it is another thing entirely. Amazing."

"A Wonderland. That's why I brought you out here," Jerry says.

"What now?"

"Just wait, my friend. We just wait. That's the beauty of

your design set up. I mean, I love the...what do you call it?" Jerry asks, pointing at some tubing running into one of the plastic pots.

"The gravity feed," I answer.

"Exactly! Let nature do all the fucking work...though we do help it somewhat. I love it. Timed lights, timed water...all hooked into the existing system. A combination 110-220 volt, some three phase pumps. It's a fucking work of art. We should get three, four crops a year. Eighty thousand clear a rotation. Hell of a lot better than wheat. And we're just following government advice. Diversify, they said. Diversify. Free market enterprise as it was meant to be. Perfect."

We push our way back through the plastic curtains into the snow and wind. Exhaust clouds nearly obscure the Bronco. Snow has nearly covered the windshield. Jerry brushes away the snow on the driver's side and steps in while Dave slides into the centre. I make a few half-hearted swipes at the passenger side window. I look back at the barn but the blowing snow forces my eyes shut. Inside Dave is flapping his arms.

"Fucking heater cut out. I just got it going again. Fucking thing," says Dave.

"Patience, my friend," whispers Jerry as he turns the truck into the lane and onto the grid road back to the city. No-one says a word until we pull to the curb in front of my apartment. Jerry turns to me. "You've created the Disneyland of hydroponics. I'm impressed. We'll talk soon. Here." Jerry hands me a thick wad of twenties. I put it in my jean pocket.

"Thanks."

"Don't spend it all in one place," says Dave.

I watch them pull away. Frankly I am glad to be rid of them. Inside my suite, I pour myself a glass of white wine and put on some Howlin' Wolf. Ever since Chicago I've been into the blues. I turn up the stereo. A year to go on the Ph.D.

I moved back here thinking it would be easier. Now what? I couldn't even bring Tanis back to the suite. I was living in a fucking gopher hole. Another dead-end relationship, another dead-end job. And then these two fucks run into my life. At least that's over now. Another year and I'm out of this town.

A few weeks later I'm at the university working in the biology lab and Jerry shows up at the window of the door. I go to the door and we stand in the hallway.

"I told you not to come here."

"Why not? 'Fraid I'll steal the best looking babes?"

"Look, I've got to get back to work. Some of these people need to get this lab done by three."

"Let them figure it out themselves. In the long run it will do them more good."

"What brings you up here?" I ask.

"We might need your help again."

"That wasn't the deal. I only did the design. Nothing more. I was very up front about that."

"Things change. We've decided it's in all of our best interests to maintain a relationship."

"A relationship? What the hell's that mean?"

"It means we have some more work to do."

"That wasn't part of the deal."

"It is now. It's back to Disney. We've got a problem. I'll pick you up just after three. Meet me on the street out front."

Jerry and I drive to the farm without speaking. He plays AC/DC on the stereo. I look out the side window of the truck, trying to lose myself in the snowdrifts on the summer fallow. I look back at the city. Clouds of steam rise over the skyline as if the entire landscape is on fire.

There is a small drift of snow in front of the barn door. We kick through it into the building. I can't help but be surprised again at the contrast. The plants have grown, and seem to vibrate in the green light. Ceiling fans circulate the heavy, humid air.

"So what's the problem?" I ask. I am starting to lose my patience.

"The water flow on this drip pipe. It doesn't seem right to me. "

He points at a spigot on one of the main water lines. A series of plastic tubes lead off the main line, constantly supplying nutrients to the plants on the metal trough.

"It looks fine to me."

"Good."

"What's that supposed to mean? I don't see any problem."

"And that's exactly what I want. No problems. I need you out here, say, once every two weeks. You know, general maintenance."

"That wasn't our arrangement. I told you, I'd design the set up. I didn't even want anything to do with the actual construction of the grow operation. I was just providing the information, the concept."

"The concept is real now, Lindsay. You can pretend all you want."

"What if I say no?"

"Don't push it, Lindsay. You've done some good work, and don't think I don't reward good work. But don't fuck it up now." Jerry zips up his leather jacket. "Time to go. I had some keys made up for you." He throws me a ring of keys. They feel cold in my hand.

The Dog has fired his entire band, which I think is a mistake because he tries to carry the show with image, and the Dog can't carry on image alone. The new group is competent. Don't get me wrong. It's just that they don't have a presence. Flat. And the blues can never be flat. The crowd feels it too. You can hear fragments of conversations while they play, which is hard to do considering the volume.

I'm sitting at the bar of Counters, half watching the band, half watching the VLTs and all the losers giving the ghost in the machine all their money. The VLTs are indiscriminate: bikers stand beside old women standing beside natives standing by guys in business suits. It's a democratic tax for the stupid. Soon I'd be playing.

I am supposed to meet Tanis at eight. It's now ten and safe to assume she is still on the computer or gone onto better things. I should check my phone messages, but the phone is by the entrance and I probably couldn't hear a thing anyways. I order another beer. The Dog is just finishing his second set.

Two girls in black tights, black T-shirts and short black leather jackets stand against the wall, each with a bottle of Heineken. Jerry leans into one of them and laughs. He looks up, sees me and waves me over. I turn back and find my reflection in the mirror. I see myself shaking my head. I get up, take my beer and walk over to the girls and Jerry.

"Good to see you," says Jerry, shaking my hand. His beer slops over our fingers as we shake hands. I wipe my hand on my jeans.

"Denise. Janelle. Lindsay." Jerry points at each of us in turn.

We all nod. The DJ kicks in with Albert King's "Born Under a Bad Sign."

"You need a toke?" asks Jerry.

"No, I'm fine."

"Yeah, you need a toot. Let's go girls." Jerry takes my arm and weaves me through the crowd milling around the bar. We turn behind the bandstand, past the open doors of the washrooms to the back hallway. Jerry nods at the bouncer lurking there. The bouncer opens the door and waves us through.

The air feels clean on my face after the smoke haze inside. Jerry lets go of my arm. He shakes his shoulders. "Beautiful," he says. It's nearly 30 below and we're standing in ankle deep snow. Jerry leans against the dumpster, taking the joint out of the top pocket of his jean jacket. He double flicks his silver

Zippo on his jeans and lights the joint. "Beautiful, man. Girls?"

He passes the joint, nodding his head at the sky. Tiny snowflakes float down, illuminated by the floodlight mounted on the top of the building. Janelle hands the joint back to Jerry.

"Lindsay?" Jerry extends the joint to me.

I take a short pull on the joint and hand it back to Jerry. He pushes my hand away. "Enjoy," he whispers.

I take another toke and hand the joint to Janelle who giggles and hands it to Denise. Jerry reaches into his jeans, takes out a twenty and hands it to Janelle. "Get a table and order a round."

"Sure. The usual?" She doesn't ask what I would like to drink. She and Denise both laugh and go back into the bar.

Jerry looks up into the light, the snow slowly falling on his face.

"We're thinking of making some changes. I think there are some opportunities we should explore."

"I've got enough opportunities right now," I say. "I'd just like to finish my degree and move on."

"Move on where, Lindsay? I'm talking large amounts here, Lindsay. Large amounts. For very little effort. Don't be a blind man."

"I don't think so, Jerry."

Jerry looks over at me, his eyes narrow slightly.

"We'll talk later. Time is a wonderful convincer," he says. He turns and goes back into the bar. I stay outside. Suddenly, I find the thought of the smoke nauseous. I turn into the back alley and start walking home. It's only when I walk up the front stairs that I realize I had left my leather jacket in the bar.

The first time I drove out to the 'farm' as Jerry calls it, I felt a rush of fear. By the second time the fear had transformed into a dull irritation. This time it's about six o'clock, midwinter, the sky already shifting to dark grey in the east. I park my ten-year-old Civic in the yard and reluctantly walk to the side door. The lock is frozen shut. I walk back to the car and find a plastic bottle of de-icer and spray the alcohol on the lock.

Inside, I spend a couple of minutes gulping in the air, feeling the warmth and humidity. The water flow is fine. I make some minor adjustments to the nutrient levels. The three foot domed metal halides are fine. Not one is burnt out, which is amazing considering they're on for over eighteen hours every day. I check the timers. Everything fine. I pass through the black plastic dividing curtain into the blooming-room. The plants are pushing out of the eight inch pots. They'd need to be transplanted soon, but that isn't my job. In here, the sodium vapours are on twelve hours a day creating a near daytime, jungle feel. If possible, the humidity is even higher.

I push through into the winter. A man in his fifties stands by my car. I hesitate in the doorway of the barn. He notices me and waves me over. I kick my way through the snow. I don't know what to say, so I simply nod at him.

"I didn't recognize the car. Thought I'd better take a look," the man says.

"It's mine. I guess you weren't around the last few times I was by."

"You know Jerry?"

"Your nephew?"

"That what he told you?"

I just nod and go to open the car door.

"Why don't you stop by the house? I've got coffee on. Warm you up for the ride."

I hesitate but say, "Sounds good to me." I don't ask his name.

At the back porch I stoop to take off my boots.

"Don't bother," he says.

Inside a trail of mud weaves through the kitchen into the living-room. Another trail leads from the couch to the bathroom. The old farmhouse is basically one room with a bathroom as an add-on. It's difficult to imagine a family living here. Boxes of newspapers and cans are piled in one corner of the kitchen section. Cartons of beer bottles are carefully stacked in another. Sheets of newspaper cover part of the floor. In the living-room are an old couch and chair with a couple of TV tables.

A huge German Shepherd comes around the corner and walks over to the man, nuzzling her head in his outstretched hands. The dog looks at me.

"I've never seen her before," I say, "Never even heard a bark. Nothing."

"This dog's a genius. Recognizes everyone. She's seen you with Jerry. To her, that means you're okay. Bring a stranger out some time. She'll go crazy."

"Amazing."

"More coffee?"

"Sure."

The man walks to the kitchen to get the pot. He has a slight limp in his right leg.

"You stay here alone?" I ask.

The man waves his right arm around the room. "What do you think?"

The room is tight. All the windows are sealed. Cigarette smoke has stained the ceiling yellow. The single light fixture is nearly brown, acting as a magnet for the smoke.

"Why?' I ask.

"You ask a lot of questions," the man says.

"I guess."

"Jerry's done some favours for me. I've done some for him. The house works for both of us. I keep an eye on things. I get a place to stay. He wanted a place for the dog. I think he moves around a lot.

"So, this wasn't your place?"

86

"You kidding me? No. I move around a lot too," the man says.

"I know what that's like," I say.

"Well, we'll be moving soon enough. Jerry's nearly finished here," says the man.

"I thought this was more permanent."

"If you're counting on this, forget it," the man says. The dogs lick his hand. I notice he is missing the first digit of his index finger. The dog is trained for motion and always keeps her eyes on me. I don't move.

I didn't go back to the farm for a few days. Nothing had ever been a problem and what was the point of worrying over nothing? I am sitting in Counters having a beer late on a Monday afternoon, trying to relax before going back to the apartment to mark the last set of lab reports, when Jerry walks in. At times he seems to know my every move.

"Hey, what's up?" he says, sitting on the next stool. He raises his chin and the bartender starts pouring him a scotch.

"Nothing," I answer. "I'm just getting ready for the next onslaught of papers."

"You need a drink then," Jerry says, raising his scotch which has already appeared. The bartender disappears leaving us alone.

Counters is always dark and quiet in the afternoons. Without people the place smells of beer and urine. A couple of bikers, not wearing their colours, sit at a corner table. An old woman is playing the VLTs, greedily smoking cigarettes and balancing a draft beer on the edge of the machine. Jerry looks over at the woman.

"Think she'll ever hit the big time?" Jerry says.

"Not very likely," I answer.

"What about you? You done any thinking about your future?" Jerry says looking straight ahead into the mirror behind the bar.

"Always thinking, constantly thinking."

"Good. Good. I've haven't seen much of you lately."

"Busy, I guess."

"Yeah, I suppose." Jerry says, signalling the bartender. "You need anything?"

"No, thanks. I've got to get going." I stand up to put on my coat and Jerry lays his hand on my forearm.

"What do you make a year?"

"Enough," I answer.

"Enough for what? I figure ten, maybe twelve thousand?"

"So?"

"You want to be a loser. You want to be like her?" Jerry points at the woman at the VLTs. "That what you want out of life?"

I don't look at him. I sip at my beer.

"You live in a hole, man. You drive shit. You drink shit."

"So? What are you getting at?"

"We've got a couple of things to discuss." Dave walks through the entrance and Jerry flags him over. "Good, a quick drink and then we're off."

Dave orders a beer. I sit down.

"We need to take a ride out to the farm this afternoon." Jerry says.

"There a problem?" I ask.

"Not sure. Better safe than sorry."

"You want me to meet you out there?" I ask.

"No, we'll all drive out together. Finished Dave?"

Dave nods, and stands up with Jerry.

"Coming?" Jerry says.

The heater in the Bronco is still acting up. It's more than 30 below and ice crystals hang in the air. I curl into myself, trying to stay warm. The horizon line is a grey smudge in front of us. Jerry turns into the yard. The house is dark, no sign of the dog. We step through the plastic into the barn. The room is completely bare. Nothing.

"What happened?" I ask.

"Time to move on," says Jerry.

"So why bring me out here?"

"Unfinished business," says Jerry. He nods at Dave who pushes his way out through the plastic screen, leaving Jerry and I alone in the room. Jerry leans against the bare wall, lighting a cigarette. Dave comes back into the room carrying a twelve-gauge shotgun.

"What's going on?" I ask.

"Ask no questions, I'll tell you no lies," says Jerry. He takes two shotgun shells from his parka, breaks the gun and inserts the shells. He snaps the barrel back together with a sudden crack.

"Come with me," says Jerry.

Dave holds the door open. Jerry leads us behind the barn. I've never been behind the barn.

"Time to deal with the powers that be," Jerry says, pointing at the back wall of the barn. There is an electric meter mounted on the wall with metal piping about five feet above the ground. Jerry hands me the shotgun.

"Blow it off," he says.

"I thought you said you weren't worried about spikes?"

"Now you know why."

"Why me?"

"Ask no questions, I'll tell you no lies. Hurry up, I'm getting cold."

Jerry and Dave move back a couple of steps. Both are smoking cigarettes and the smoke seems to hang in the air surrounding them in the dull grey light. Jerry points at the meter. I turn around, and lift the gun. Even through my gloves my fingers feel numb holding the cold metal. I lift the gun and fire. In the still air, the roar is deafening. Glass and wood splinter in a cloud, settling on the snow. Jerry reaches out and takes the gun, cracking it open and stuffing two more shells in before snapping it shut.

"Now we talk about you."

"What about me?"

"I'm worried. I offer you an opportunity, a golden opportunity, and you fuck it up. I don't know. What is it? You think you're better than anyone else? You think you can sit back and pass judgment on the world?"

"Look, I just don't want to get too involved, okay?"

"Okay? You still think there are different degrees of being involved? You think you can watch the world, like you're sitting on some fucking barstool, watching the rest of the room through the mirror? You don't think I watch you. You don't think you're involved?"

"Okay, I'm involved. Is that what you want to hear? I'm involved, okay?"

"You're learning." Jerry lifts up the gun. He waves it past my eyes.

"Are you going to shoot me?"

Jerry starts laughing, waving the gun at the sky. Dave joins in, their laughter echoing in the yard. "Fuck no. What do you think this is? Alabama? We need to go for a ride."

We walk around to the Bronco. I sit jammed in between Jerry and Dave, who is driving this time. Jerry doesn't put the gun in the back and instead sits with it between his legs, barrel pointed up and aimed toward the window. At the end of the lane Dave turns the truck away from the city. We drive on. Disneyland disappears. Jerry opens the glove compartment and retrieves a mickey of rye. He takes a pull on the bottle, and hands it to Dave who also takes a long swallow. Dave passes me the bottle.

"Have a shot Lindsay," says Jerry. I shake my head, but he pushes the bottle at me. I take a small sip and move to hand the bottle back. Jerry pushes my hand back. "Have another."

A Boat in Still Water

I took the elevator from my office floor to the ground level, turned the corner and then took the escalator to the subway level. It was three stops on the 2 Express to the labyrinth of Penn Station. I had packed a small travel bag at my apartment in the morning, and carried it with a brief case containing the manuscript I was currently editing—an academic text on the influence of the flaneur on the modern European novel. The text was difficult, and I was starting to feel like a detached observer myself. Maybe a few days away from Manhattan would help.

The train was already fifteen minutes late. I found an empty bench and read the Times. Some of the upscale homeless had slipped through the security gate. A man across from me sang quietly to himself, looking up anxiously at the security guard by the information booth. Another man quickly went through the garbage, eventually finding a half eaten piece of chicken and some French fries. An old woman folded her Washington Post and looked at both men with disdain. Her newspaper was over a week old and covered with food stains. The headlines mentioned Bush and the Savings and Loans scandals. I was already starting to get tired of the 1980's, and we were only half way through the decade. The commuters heading back into Connecticut stood by the newspaper stand, or waited by the information clock outside the 'ticket necessary' section.

Trains have always made me feel like I was on a great voyage, even if the journey was only a few hours. There was something about the hypnotic power of the sound of metal moving on metal, and the immediate passing of landscape that shifted me into a different time. I was leaving New York, the heat and humidity, the stifling cubicle office space, streets I was weary of walking, and a relationship that was going nowhere fast. I found it strange that Alice was the one who recommended I spend a few days in Mystic with Rhonda, an old friend of a friend. We had been together two years since I had moved to New York from Chicago, after meeting a couple of times at backyard BBQs in Brooklyn with the sound of Italian opera and firecrackers echoing in the inner space of the brownstones. I wondered what Alice was thinking.

Rhonda was waiting in a new black Accord in the lot of the Mystic train station. When she saw me she got out of the car and kissed me. She smiled. I thought I knew that look. She didn't look at me like a friend. She opened the trunk for my bags.

"Can you drive? We're meeting some friends at the club. That okay with you?" Rhonda asked.

"I have absolutely no plans," I answered. She gave me directions through town, pointing out places with quick jabs of her index finger. She pointed out Mystic Pizza.

"That's where I first got sick of what's her name."

On the main street we waited as a bridge lifted and three yachts went through the channel to the open water of the harbour.

"People schedule their day by the bridge. There is a schedule for the raising and lowering. It can tie up traffic for hours. I always make sure I'm never around when it's operating," she said.

"Why are we here then?"

"I thought you might want to see it."

"Oh," I said.

The private yacht club had a long wooden deck overlooking the boat docks. Fresh flowers were on every marble table, resting in cut glass vases.

Rhonda ordered a Long Island ice tea. I ordered a white wine. "May I recommend the California Chardonnay. It's especially lovely," said the waitress.

"Sounds fine to me."

The harbour was beautiful. I listened to the halyards ringing like chimes in the wind. The waitress brought our drinks just as Rhonda's friend, Janice, arrived. Janice nodded in the general direction of the outdoor bar. A bartender dressed in black and white immediately bent to his work. My wine glass glowed golden in the sunlight. The waitress brought three martinis. Janice lined them up in front of one another in a straight row on the marble top. She drank them one after the other.

"Perfect," she said after the third martini. "The day looks much brighter now. And much, much drier."

"Good," said Rhonda. "This is Ray. He's up from New York for a couple of days.

"Seeing the sights of the big city? Right. Mystic Seaport. Make sure he eats at Mystic Pizza," Janice said. She signalled the waitress and started to laugh.

"We might skip some of the highlights," said Rhonda. I looked at her as she spoke. She had a gorgeous smile. I quickly looked away and picked up a newspaper Janice had dropped on the table. There was a small article on page two, announcing a nuclear submarine launch the next day.

"I'd actually like to see this," I said.

"What? Read it," said Janice.

"'Electric Boat, a division of General Dynamics, wishes to announce the launching ceremony of the latest attack submarine, the SSN 757, attack submarine, Alexandria,' " I read.

"Why would you want to see that?" asked Rhonda.

"Curiosity I suppose."

"More like a male interest in huge phallic weapons. Little boys comparing pee pees." said Janice. "I hope you realize how incredibly tedious those things are."

"I don't have to worry. It says it's closed to the general public, by special authorized invitation only," I said.

"Fuck it. You want to go?" Janice dug into her purse and

threw two green tickets at me. "My ex works as an engineer for Electric Boat. They sent the invitations to the wrong address. If you see him, say fuck you very much from all of us. Fuck him. You interested in dinner? Why not stop over for a hot tub?"

"Tomorrow might be better," said Rhonda. "Ray's going to be in town a couple of days. There'll be time to get together."

"Sure. Time. That's something I've got plenty of," said Janice, leaning back in her chair. She looked out at the yachts. "I wonder if that bastard is sailing again today."

"Let it go," said Rhonda.

"Yeah. Let it go," said Janice.

Rhonda's house was on the other side of Mystic. The Honda was making a strange sound she said and she wanted to know what I thought. It sounded fine to me, but I pretended to be concerned.

"Don't mind Janice. The divorce will be final in a couple of months and then she can get on with her life. I had the same problems. After the papers are signed, it makes a difference. Maybe tomorrow night we can spend some time with her."

"Whatever you've got planned is fine with me."

"Divorce is bizarre. It's like an epidemic. All these fucking men. It's like they get a contagious disease. And they leave all at once. Years of time together and then you instantly become strangers. You sure you don't hear something? He wanted me to have this car. He took the van and his motorcycle. I don't trust him."

"At least you had no kids," I said.

"Thank god. Though we divide everything up like children. He gets the stocks. I get the house. He gets the new babe. I get the grief. Fuck him. And I'm tired of everyone saying everything works out. I'm going to turn the house into a bed and breakfast and work the tourist thing. Speaking about tourists, you want to see Mystic Seaport? I've got a friend working PR who can probably get you in.

"Worth seeing?"

"If you like ships, yeah. This used to be a whaling port. If you're into history you'd probably find it interesting, though I have to admit it's a bit touristy."

"We'll see," I said.

Back at the house I started rethinking. Actually touristy might be perfect. I was dreading working through the galley proofs. I'd go through seaports, eat pizza, anything to avoid them. I thought of calling Alice, but she knew where I was. It wasn't as if we weren't getting along. It was more like an if-neither-of-us-rocked-the-boat-we-could-keep-sailing state of inaction. I felt the same way about my work, about everything. A boat in still waters. I was going nowhere.

"What about dinner?" Rhonda asked.

"Isn't it famous for lobster here?"

"Okay, but I'm sick of lobster. The price dropped so much I was eating it once a week. Turn left here. We'll stop at Tom's place."

Tom lived in a small silver trailer parked in a hollow near the shore of a large inlet. Three golden retrievers bounded up to the car, barking loudly, as we pulled into the gravel side road by the trailer. A woman, carrying a puppy came to the car window.

"Hi, Denise. Tom around?" asked Rhonda.

"He's out back puttering with the outboard," said Denise. "Come on in and get some coffee."

The trailer was cluttered with coils of rope and stacks of newspapers. Denise cleared an area on the couch for us and went to the kitchen counter and poured three cups of coffee. "Sorry, there's no cream or sugar."

"Black is fine," I said.

"This is Ray. Lives in New York,"

"Manhattan?"

"Brooklyn, actually," I said.

"Good, a real person. I hate those flakes from the city. They come up here, find it quaint, buy the fucking place and change everything. Soon there'll be no room for any of us," said Denise, lighting a cigarette. "What's up? Heard from that jerk of a husband?"

"Only through my lawyer," said Rhonda.

"Probably better that way. What's up with you, Ray?" said Denise.

"Not much," I said, not really knowing what she meant.

"What do you do in Brooklyn?"

"I edit...books mainly," I said.

"I read a book once," said Denise.

Tom came in. He was wearing jeans and a denim shirt.

"Hey, Rhonda. What's up?"

"Tom. Ray." We shook hands. "We need two or three good sized lobsters. What you got?"

"I haven't checked the traps yet. Too damned busy with the damned motor. Seized again. You want to pick them out?" asked Tom.

"Sure," said Rhonda.

Tom, Rhonda and I walked down to the water's edge. Tom pushed a small rowboat into the water and he and Rhonda rowed out to a red buoy about twenty yards into the inlet. Tom hauled up a wooden trap. They pulled lobsters from the traps, holding each up to the sky, judging weight and colour. Tom and Rhonda laughed, the sound echoing across the water. I stood in the sand on the edge of the water.

Tom rowed back to shore, pausing so Rhonda could pluck some eel grass from the water.

Rhonda carried the metal pail over to me. "What do you think?" she said. Three lobsters lay tangled in the eel grass.

"Perfect," I said.

I'm amazed by some people in the kitchen. Alice and I were both the work late types. Our idea of cooking was thinking up different take out ideas. Rhonda was one of those magician types who could make anything out of nothing. No Woody Allen scene here. She was incredibly proficient. She boiled water in a huge stainless steel stockpot. As the water boiled she cut vegetables, heated garlic bread, made and heated garlic butter. I sat on a bar stool by the breakfast ledge.

"Are you sure?"

"No, don't ask again. You could pour me another glass of wine," Rhonda said.

The white wine was on the ledge by my elbow. I reached over, pulling the bottle out of the thermos ice bucket and poured her a glass as she reached over from the island.

"Thanks." She took a quick sip of wine and immediately went back to making a cheese sauce for the cauliflower.

"Why no kids?" I asked.

"Lucky, I guess, thank God. A husband was difficult enough. But that, as they say, is all in the past. You never been married?"

"No."

"What about Alice?"

"Nothing so far." I poured myself another glass of wine. We were getting into drinking territory. "I'm not sure where the relationship is going."

"That's what Alice mentioned."

"Really?"

The water in the stockpot was boiling. Rhonda placed some of the eel grass in the water and then slowly she lifted the three lobsters, one at a time, dropping them into the boiling water. I thought I heard a thin squealing sound, but it was probably only the water splashing as the lobsters displaced the space.

We sat in the silence. Rhonda drank her wine and I listened for sounds of suffering. I only heard the steady boiling of water. Fifteen minutes passed. I know. I watched the clock.

"I think everything is ready," Rhonda said.

The lobsters were delicious, succulent and rich. We didn't talk. Instead we drank another bottle of white wine from upstate New York, which was surprisingly good. Rhonda looked beautiful in the candlelight. There was a quiet grace in her movements.

We cleared the dishes, moving around each other in the kitchen. I poured us each another glass of wine and we sat at the cleared table. Rhonda looked out the window. The glass threw reflections back at her. She turned to me and smiled.

"Coffee?" she asked.

"No, thanks."

"Good. It would just keep you up," said Rhonda. "More wine?"

"I'm fine really."

Rhonda poured herself another glass of wine.

"I don't know why I drink this stuff. Probably because of my husband. He's a serious alcoholic. Occupational hazard around here."

"Really."

"Same with Janice's husband," said Rhonda.

"What about Janice?"

Rhonda just looked at me. "Are you going to tell me about Alice?"

"What's there to tell?"

"You tired?"

"I hate to admit it, but yeah, I am," I said.

"You can share the bed with me or take the couch in the other room."

"You have a preference?" I asked.

"Whatever you want."

"Maybe I should sleep on the couch."

"Your choice. There are sheets, blankets, whatever you need in the closet."

She went into the bathroom and I pulled the sheets and blankets from the closet and started making up the couch.

When I looked up Rhonda came out of the bathroom, wearing only a long white T-shirt. She leaned against the arm of the couch.

"Anything you need before you sleep?"

"No, I'm fine."

She nodded, then stood up and slowly went to the bedroom door. When she opened the door the light framed her. She turned toward me.

"Good night," she said and shut the bedroom door.

The living-room was in semi-darkness. There was a thin line of light coming from under her bedroom door. I sat in the large chair across from her door. I poured myself another glass of wine and went out to the back deck, which overlooked a sloping meadow, then a line of trees. On the other side of the trees was the ocean. I couldn't see it, but I could smell the salt in the air as the wind came off the water. I stood for a long time staring into the dark space beyond the trees.

I finished my coffee in the car as we drove the few miles to the town of Groton on the other side of Mystic. Rhonda dropped me off down the block from the gate.

"You sure you don't want to come?" I said.

"I hate this place. I'm not going any closer," said Rhonda. "Military idiots."

"Who's that?" I pointed at a small crowd carrying placards at the end of the block.

"Protesters. They come for every launch. Not that it does any good."

"I'll call when it's over," I said.

She turned the corner. I was on a long street lined with low wooden buildings, most of them bars or cafes. Across the street ran a high wire fence, capped with razor wire. There was another wire fence behind it, creating a sort of no man's land between the two. There was a security gate with several guards. A crowd of people funnelled into the entrance, all holding green passes. I looked at my pass, printed with diagonal submarine silhouettes and approached the gate. I expected a heavy security check. Instead a fat man in a badly fitting uniform looked at my ticket and told me to enjoy myself.

I walked down a wire-fenced passageway to another gate. There were several posters warning of the dangers of mercury poisoning. Guards with automatic weapons and Rottweilers lined the entrance into a larger area where the main crowd was huddled in the shadows of the colossal hulls of three unfinished nuclear submarines. Someone next to me said they were Tridents, nearly 600 feet long. I stopped walking to stare at them. Two were already named: the *Maryland*, the *Nebraska*, the third, painted in dull red undercoating was not yet lettered.

Someone pushed me from behind and I passed into the larger area where a heavy-set woman in a bright red apron printed with "I Cooked for EB" stood behind an enormous black grill. I felt a push on my shoulder. I turned and a man nodded.

"What do you think?" the man said, pointing back at the hull of the Nebraska.

"Big," I said.

"I'll say. I riveted the fucker."

"Really?"

"Weeks and weeks, every single one had to be inspected and okayed. Don't want it to do a Titanic first time out. Too fucking embarrassing," the man said. he turned to the woman serving hamburgers "Give me another cheeseburger."

"The American way," I said.

"Fucking rights. This is worth fighting for. I wish they served Coke," he said. "You?"

"Doesn't really matter," I said.

"Not a fighting man? Hey, sorry, I'm not too civilized today, or any day for that matter. My name's Earl, like Earl the Pearl."

"Ray," I said.

Earl tucked his cheeseburger and Pepsi to his left hand and shook my hand.

"Pleasure to meet you," Earl said. "Get yourself a burger. They're damn good."

"The woman handed me a hamburger covered in onions and a slice of processed cheese. "Sorry," she said, "We're out of Pepsi."

"Then get him a Coke," said Earl.

"This is fine thanks," I said, but the woman had already turned away.

A brass band was playing military marches on a small stage covered with plenty of red, white and blue bunting. Flags surrounded the stage area. "Come on," said Earl, "Let's make our way to the front. I love listening to this bullshit." Earl started pushing his way through the crowd and I followed in his wake.

Behind the stage and to the right was the new submarine, sleek and jet black. The crew stood at stiff attention on the deck. In the conning tower the officers were rigid under the flags. A woman in a white dress stood beside them.

On the stage a politician type was giving one of those 'don't let us be fooled by events in the East' speeches. "There are still Reds everywhere and we need deterrents like this attack submarine to keep those people in line with America," the politician said and the crowd went wild. Earl rolled his eyes, "Those people barely know their way out of bed."

The politician sat down and a chaplain stood up to bless the ship. Finally a woman in a bright red dress approached the submarine carrying a champagne bottle. She swung the bottle like a baseball batter and missed the submarine. She laughed and swung again, making contact, white foam running down the hull. A harbour horn blared and the crowd surged forward to watch the huge black cylinder of the submarine slide down the launching ramp into the harbour, creating a wave, which washed back on shore. The boat bobbed quietly in the still water, the crew still in stiff crease salutes.

The woman in the party dress waved briefly at someone in the crowd and then stood perfectly still beside the captain.

The General Dynamics security guards let the crowd watch for a few minutes and then started pressing the crowd back to the compound gates, Earl and I at the end of the line.

"Show's over," said Earl, "They don't waste much time."

"Subtle," I answered. Behind me two Rottweilers on thick chains sniffed at my legs. The guards holding them refused to look at me and kept advancing until we were back under the three unfinished Tridents.

Earl tapped me on the shoulder. "Think about it. Each of those mothers holds 192 warheads. They want these babies finished before the next election. It's all dollars and nonsense and politics."

"In what order?" I said.

The crowd passed through the chain link gates, past the security guard boxes. Most of them piled into waiting cars or walked to the corner. Across the street just outside the gates was a row of dilapidated bars.

"Party's over," said Earl. "Let's get a beer."

I couldn't see any sign of Rhonda.

"I'm supposed to meet someone," I said.

"Call them from inside. Let's go," said Earl.

The bars were mostly ramshackle clapboard buildings with names like El Bolero, Gap's and Gap's Too, Fast Attack News and Deli, Elfe's Cafe, Rag's Liquor Cafe. We went into Gap's Too. Inside the door, I couldn't see Earl in the gloom and cigarette smoke. I finally found him standing at the long wooden bar on the other side of the pool table. I wove my way past a guy lining up a shot, pausing as he pulled back the cue. I joined Earl, wedging myself between a couple of heavy-set men wearing denim jeans and vests. Several neon beer signs made the air glow. A black "POW MIA You are not Forgotten" flag hung on the wall behind the bar above the potato chip bags.

"Budweiser, the breakfast of champions," Earl said,

handing me a beer.

"Thanks. You seem to know your way around here," I said.

"I should. Twenty five years in that plant. I've seen everyone and everything."

"I believe it."

"What brings you here?" asked Earl.

"Curiosity," I said.

Earl took a long pull on his beer. "Curiosity killed the cat," he said.

"Good thing I'm not a cat."

"Yeah, good thing," said Earl.

There were several televisions in the bar all tuned to different stations. Groups of guys clustered around the various screens. A TV in the corner above the bar, in a break during the Yankee game, showed a commercial for lawyers, "for best results call, 1-800-99-Court." On another, two huge men in bright costumes were wrestling, while another screen showed rock videos.

"You like the show?" asked Earl.

"The show?"

"Yeah, the show. They bring out the band, all the local politicians, free food and then wham! It's over. You know what I mean?"

"About the launch?"

"Gives us another couple of beers," Earl yelled at the bar man. "What do you think I'm talking about?"

"It's an impressive ship," I said.

"A boat. A submarine is a boat. No-one knows the difference anymore."

I didn't answer. I went to pay for the beers, but Earl pushed my hand away. "I'll get it. My show, my dollar."

"The day-to-day work is nothing like that. We put in twelve hours shifts sometimes pulling overtime. Lunch breaks. Wham! We're over here. Beer and shots for half an hour, then back to work."

"Must wear you out," I said.

"Exactly," said Earl. "What kind of work you do?"

"I edit," I said.

"Edit? Edit what?"

"Books mainly, the occasional article."

"Books? What kind of books?"

"Fiction mainly," I said.

"The kind people like to read?"

"Occasionally."

"Fiction. Perfect. Listen, truth is stranger than fiction believe me, you'd better fucking well believe me," said Earl. "I could tell you stories you fucking wouldn't believe, fucking right man."

"I believe you Earl. Listen, I should make that phone call," I said.

"Phone's right at the back by the can. Take a piss, save yourself a trip later. Two more beers!"

The toilet was disgusting. There was no paper, of course. I wiped my hands on my jeans digging through my pockets for the scrap of paper with Rhonda's cell number.

"Hi, Rhonda?" I could hear traffic in the background.

"Where you been? You want me to pick you up?"

"Please."

"Look for me on the corner in five. We're seeing Janice tonight."

"Can't wait. See you in five."

Earl had finished his beer and was starting on mine when I got back to the bar. He looked up and smiled. "Two more," he yelled. "Now, you want stories? You're a writer, right? "

"Someday. Now, I edit writers," I said.

"Same difference. Listen, you might learn something." He took another long drink of his beer. "You know there's a guy up on the coast, Maine or something. Probably Bangor, some place like that. You know what his job is? All day, you know what he does?"

"No."

"Sits in a metal cylinder under the water, somewhere under the ocean or something, with his finger on the trigger. Think about it. Nothing but him in a tube in the water. Like the finger of judgment, on a fucking button. Whacked out probably, I mean sensory deprivation, god knows what kind of drugs. You know what I mean? The final step and you know how many times he's pushed it?

"You mean the same guy? All the time?"

"I don't know. Maybe they work shifts. I heard this from a friend who does some welding in the navy. Big stuff. He said he met this guy in a bar, so I guess they must work shifts or something."

"How many times?" I asked.

"Three, three fucking times, but we're okay 'cause there has to be two, you know what I mean? Three fucking times. It's a mother fucking world, man."

"I'll say. Listen I've got to go. Great talking to you," I said.

"Hey, one more for the road," said Earl.

I stood up. There was a wallet under Earl's chair. I bent down and picked it up. "This yours?"

Earl patted his ass. "Yeah, thanks. Let me buy you a beer."

"No, I'm fine. I'm out of here."

"Remember, Ray. It's a mother fucking world."

"You're right, Earl."

The sunlight was blinding after the gloom of the bar. It was barely noon. It seemed much later. That always happens when I drink beer early in the day. Rhonda was parked at the corner and I walked over and opened the passenger's door.

"You want to drive?"

"No, I'm fine."

"Interested in lunch?"

"I've already eaten."

"Back there? Are you insane or just stupid?"

"Either one probably describes me well."

"I'm thinking of taking my niece to a movie, interested?"

"No, I'm a little wiped out actually," I said.

"Too much military bullshit, I'd say," said Rhonda.

"Probably."

"Well, I've promised her. You want me to drop you at the Seaport?

"No, the launch was enough excitement for me. I'm feeling guilty about the manuscripts. I really should make an effort to at least get started."

"Fine with me. I'll drop you at the house. Just remember we're going over to Janice's tonight for supper and maybe a hot tub."

"Sounds good to me."

After she drove off I made another pot of coffee and took a lawn chair from the porch. I found some shade on the back lawn overlooking the trees and took out my manuscripts and coffee. I pointed my chair in the general direction of the water. If I listened carefully I could hear the ocean. I only read for a few minutes before I fell asleep.

At Janice's we ate take-out Mystic Pizza and drank Coronas in the kitchen. Janice said all the tourists eat the pizza since the movie. I hadn't seen the movie. She smoked cigarettes while she ate, leaving all the crusts and the ash in a heap on a plate in the middle of the table. The house was incredibly large and empty since her husband had left her last year. If one walked down the road there was a marvellous view of the ocean from two sides. She got the house in the divorce settlement. He got the stock options and his share in a condo in New York. He still has to pay her $110,000 to even things out, but the money is in escrow.

The hot tub was on a raised platform in the master bedroom on the second floor. A skylight opened above us. Candles lit the room.

"I wonder what the bastard is doing now?" said Janice.

"Who cares? Good riddance," said Rhonda.

"You know, I'd like to make love with him just once

more."

"You've got to be kidding."

"Yeah and then just when he's ready to come, push him away and laugh. See what you're missing you stupid bastard?" She poured another glass of champagne and lit another cigarette though she still had a one lit in the ashtray. "Fuck him. Fuck all men."

I decided not to argue the point.

"Did you two bring bathing suits?"

I looked at Rhonda. She was already taking off her clothes.

"It's fine with me," Janice said. She stood naked beside the tub. "It's a little hot, but you'll get used to it."

I stood beside the tub suddenly feeling like a little kid. They were both beautiful. I turned slightly, took off my clothes and got in the tub. I felt like I was entering a hormone pool.

"There, that's better," said Janice, pouring another glass of champagne. "My fantasy is to drink champagne with a man in the hot tub. I would have a VCR right by the tub and then we could watch really tacky porn movies. You know the kind I mean, no story, just lots of fucking," said Janice.

Janice leaned over the tub edge to get another glass of champagne. Her right breast rested on the top of the hot tub. She poured from the bottle, spilling champagne into the tub. Beside me, Rhonda leaned back against the edge of the tub. Beads of perspiration made her face glow in the candle light. I leaned back against the edge of the tub and watched the pin pricks of stars through the skylight.

We walked across the meadow to Rhonda's house in silence. Instead of entering the house, Rhonda sat in one of the deck chairs. She leaned back and looked into the sky.

"Do you ever look at the stars anymore?"

I leaned against the railing of the deck breathing in the night air. The wind moved clouds across the sky like a hand wiping a slate clean.

"In Montana the sky was enormous. I rarely notice the stars in New York. Too many lights."

"You still in the Heights?"

"It's a good compromise. Good access. Good restaurants."

"Do you always compromise?"

"What do you mean?"

"You don't have to leave tomorrow you know."

"I should get back,"

"To Alice?"

"Alice. Work."

"I have to drive up to Boston to sign some papers tomorrow. The entire house is yours. You could probably finish the manuscripts in a day or two. And maybe start on something you really want to do."

"What do you mean?"

"You know what I think? I think you're waiting for a wind to blow you somewhere. Any place. It's really very simple. It's all about choices."

I turned from the railing. "I just want to thank you for everything," I said.

Rhonda didn't say anything. I moved toward her to give her a hug. We held each other in the stillness, listening to each other's breath. She moved her head back slightly and I leaned forward and kissed her. Her hands traced the line of my shoulder blade.

I let go and moved back to the deck railing.

"I'm sorry," I said.

"For what?"

"I don't know."

She shook her head and moved to the door. "The offer is still open. Let me know."

Rhonda went inside and I was left in the immense darkness. I watched the moon appear through the clouds. I shut my eyes. I couldn't hear any traffic and when the wind shifted I could faintly hear the ocean. I went inside and laid out my clothes for tomorrow. I packed the manuscripts in case I decided to leave. I would decide tomorrow. I was asleep in minutes.

The sound of a key rattled in the front door lock. The door swung open and Janice entered. She carried a half empty bottle of champagne.

"Shhhh," she said, "Don't wake Rhonda." She held up the key. "One of the benefits of house-sitting."

"What are you doing here?" I asked.

"Visiting," she said. "I wanted you to feel at home. Why don't you get a glass?"

"No, thanks," I said.

"I meant for me," she said.

"I'm sure you know where they are."

"Sarcastic. I could learn to like that." She took a drink from the bottle and tossed her hair. "Mind if I make myself more comfortable? Good." She took off her T-shirt. She wasn't wearing a bra. "You sure you don't want any?"

"No."

"Too bad. It's French and very, very cold."

She took another drink and took off the rest of her clothes leaving them in a pile beside the sofa. "I'm cold," she said. She sat on the edge of the sofa, leaned forward and touched my hair.

"Fuck me," she whispered.

I moved away, and she moved into the space. I pushed away, but she wrapped her legs around me. Tangled in the sheet it was difficult to move. "I don't think this is a great idea," I said.

"No? Why not? Fuck me." She moved her hand under the blankets. I pushed her away.

"You're drunk," I said.

"No kidding. You're a fucking genius." And she was asleep, just like that, but still holding on tight. Instead of pushing her away and risking waking her, I just gave in and tried my best to make myself comfortable. Janice lay warm and soft beside me. I listened to her breath. I fought having an erection. I thought of many things. I thought of Alice back in New York. I thought of Rhonda in the next room. I thought of light through a skylight. I thought of all those nuclear missiles under the sea, playing hide and seek in a world of children. And the next morning I no longer cared when Rhonda walked in and found us tangled up like fish in a net.

Ain't Gonna Be Your Dog

"Do you have any idea how much I'm going to lose in tips tonight? Saturday is always my best night," said Sarah. She lit a cigarette and blew the smoke at me.

"I thought we'd agreed you wouldn't smoke in the truck," I said.

"That was before you ruined my Saturday."

"You didn't have to come. I told you that."

"Right. And never hear the end of it."

I opened the butterfly window. It was early winter and snow had already filled the ditches. The winter air felt like cold water on my face.

"And close that fucking window. It's freezing in here."

"Then put out your cigarette," I said.

"Fine." She butted the cigarette in the ashtray, which held my parking change. "Sorry. I thought it was an ashtray."

I closed the window. I could still feel cold air on my legs rushing in through the rust holes.

"And do we have to listen to that all the time?" Sarah pointed at the cassette player.

"Howling Wolf? You don't like the blues?"

"I get enough of it at work. Bikers love that shit," said Sarah. "And when are you going to get rid of that cassette player? You're from the fucking Stone Age."

"I call it retro, sweetheart."

I turned down the music. The old Chess recordings made the hair on my neck stand on end.

"Have I met these people before?"

"Once. In the mall."

"I can't remember."

"They won't either."

I crossed the freeway and turned onto the grid to Gary's acreage. The gravel kicked up under the van sounding like a

Latin band. I looked over at Sarah. She was staring straight ahead. She was blonde and quite beautiful in the winter light. She had a small scar on her left eyebrow. Yet another mystery. How well did I really know this woman? We'd been seeing each other for almost two years. I had met her at a theatre party when I had painted the sets for a Fringe production. My only real venture into the arts. Otherwise the closest I got to art was some sponge painting and stencilling for some trendy clients. Sarah had a small part in the play. I can't remember the title. She had just quit Theatre School in Montreal and moved back to town. We stayed together for the next few weeks, alternating between her tiny bachelor apartment and my small house in Fairhaven. Sarah and I had what could only be described as a steamy relationship. The sex was great but not much else. In fact nothing else.

I painted houses during the day, and she worked nights at three different bars, though she fancied herself as an actor. Most of her hours were at the Barbarian, one of the many strange little places that kept popping up in narrow leased spaces in strip malls and office complexes. The place was designed for guys coming off the job sites who wanted three or four quick shots before they went home to the wife and three kids in the rented apartment complex, the guys who moved from job to job, following the building booms. I knew all about the booms. I had followed them from Edmonton to Vancouver to Kelowna to Calgary and back to Saskatoon—my Western Canadian tour of beer and work and rock and roll. My wife had decided to jump off the ride in Vancouver, or 'LaLa Land' as some of my friends called it. She said if she was going to be broke she wanted the sea and no winter. She said she didn't want to end up a loser like me. She said I was going nowhere. She was probably right, though I would go somewhere if I had a clue where to go. Instead I stayed on for the ride. Vancouver rain wasn't my idea of paradise. As long as I stayed moving, I felt like I was getting somewhere. Even now I still commuted to Calgary for the occasional job, driving 400 miles to paint the interior of a house if the money was there.

I turned off the grid into Gary's lane. Gary, his wife Linda and two kids lived in an unfinished pseudo-Colonial monster house with lots of filigree and narrow carved wooden columns. Gary was a house contractor who had recently developed a couple of sub divisions. Despite this ability to organize and complete large projects he never found the time or energy to finish his own house though they had lived there for over fifteen years. The siding had only been completed on two sides of the house and parts of the roof didn't even have eaves troughs. Metal storm fencing formed three connected pens for their German Shepherds, who all commenced barking as we turned into the gravel drive. I parked by the three-car garage at the back of the house. One of the metal doors was bent in a deep convex dent where Linda had backed the van.

"Quite the place," said Sarah.

"It's got a lot of potential."

"So does a plugged toilet. It's all about potential."

Behind the house was a concrete block building with several small metal pens in front of it. The kennel, a drop off point in these travel disjointed times for doting owners who only wanted the best for their babies, was another of Gary's part-time business ventures. Linda had taken over the day-to-day running of it when Gary lost momentum. The dogs inside started answering the Shepherds. The barking was deafening.

Gary and Linda had started raising German Shepherds in their spare time. Gary thought it would be a good way to earn money and keep involved in the kennel. They started giving obedience classes and breeding classes and police dog training and grooming classes. Their spare time became all the time. In fact Gary and Linda had become dog people. Dog people lived life vicariously through their dogs. They travel with their dogs, they eat with their dogs, they sleep with their dogs. They travel in packs with other dog people, partying, socializing—constantly talking about their dogs like middle-aged boomer mothers at a trendy coffee house.

Gary was a hustler, always working a new angle, though never having the time to devote enough time to finish any one project. Besides his building and developing business he sold Watkins. She sold Mary Kay. He also sold a designer line of pet foods. The latest venture was a pet crematorium. They cremated the animals in a kiln in a field across from the kennel. Gary tried to cover all the angles. Somehow he managed to keep his construction business separate from his other myriad business schemes. Linda acted as secretary taking calls, usually forgetting to pass on the messages. The building business prospered, everything else floundered in a sea of confusion.

Sarah and I walked through a side door into the garage. Inside was an old badly dented station wagon, probably Linda's. The floor was piled high with firewood and old furniture. Oil stained the concrete floor like ancient maps. We knocked at a side door and listened to more barking.

"Beautiful," said Sarah.

Linda yelled, "Come on in. They won't hurt you." I opened the back door leading into a hall and a young Shepherd jumped up at me, barking and sniffing me in a frenzy. Sarah stood behind me in the garage. I pushed them down and the dogs moved back into the hallway, the floor covered with muddy newspapers.

"Leave your shoes on," I said.

"No kidding," said Sarah. We knocked the snow off our boots and walked down the hall into the living-room, stepping over the dog sprawled in the doorway. The floors were plywood with no floor covering at all. Huge chunks had been torn out where the dogs had chewed on the floor. German Shepherds love to eat plywood. At least Gary's German Shepherds love to eat plywood. It's a strange sight to see tooth marks on a floor. The dogs' claws had also torn up the flooring, if four by eight sheets of 3/4 inch plywood can be termed flooring. The edges of the stairs were in tatters. Walking across the living-room in socks was a nightmare.

The room had an enormous vaulted ceiling with great southern lighting. The walls were still naked sheet rock. I had offered to paint the interior several times but Gary never seemed to get the sheet rock taped. Gary rarely seemed to get anything done on this house. he either had ran out of energy or he enjoyed the chaos of a building site. I knew that he had stacked the Italian tile and oak hardwood for the entire house in the garage five years ago. He said he wanted to finish the painting first.

Gary and Linda had designed the interior in 'early college coed.' The furniture could have come from a Salvation Army thrift store. I'm sure some of it did because that's exactly where I had got the couch I gave them before I had moved to Vancouver. The couch was worn out then and I hadn't felt it worth my while to haul it half way across the country. The arms were now ragged from the dog's chewing on them and white stuffing protruded through the holes.

Scarf, the current stud German Shepherd, came out from behind the sofa. He was massive. Gary had him flown over from Germany two years ago and had made a fortune using the dog as a stud for the local dog clubs. Scarf approached me and didn't bark. He sniffed at my legs. I slowly extended the back of my hand so he could catalogue me in his primal brain. Then he lay back down beside the sofa.

Keith, their fifteen-year-old son, lay on a black bean bag chair in the middle of the plywood floor. He was engrossed in some action video and didn't look up.

I hadn't been in the house for over a year. Not much had changed. The stereo cabinet was covered with dog trophies. There was a pile of cassettes and CDs on the floor.

"We'll just be a minute. Gary's out in the kennel. Make yourself at home," Linda yelled from the kitchen.

Sarah looked around the room and then at me. She raised both hands upward and shrugged her shoulders.

"Try the sofa," I said.

"Not likely," she said.

I sunk deep into the sofa and felt something digging in me. I reached back, grabbed a rawhide bone and threw it on the floor. The young Shepherd raced to the bone but when Scarf snarled he moved away immediately.

"How do you know these people?" Sarah asked.

"Through work. Gary's a contractor. When he does a project he calls me."

"Slum lord specials. I mean, look at this place."

"He's actually very good," I said.

"I bet," said Sarah.

I had been working for Gary for several years, painting the interiors of the houses in the new sub divisions. I was fast and worked off the books to keep our accounting simple. What the government didn't know wouldn't hurt them. Gary's last project had kept me busy most of the winter. I had made enough so I didn't have to commute to Calgary or Edmonton. I also had made enough for a down payment on a small bungalow in Fairhaven.

When he had called about dinner I thought he was finally calling about a new project. Lately I had been doing a run on kitchens for some reason and I was really hoping he had some work for me. I hate working around other people's stuff. That's why I like working for Gary—all the interiors were bare, bare walls and floors, no junk or memories to clutter the purity of the space. I loved coming in right after the drywallers were finished and the smell of the plaster and tape was fresh in the closed rooms. Dinner was another matter. Usually when he called I would said I was busy. I'm not sure why I agreed this time, and to add to the situation, an evening with Sarah was always an adventure.

The front door opened and Gary walked in wearing a ripped

parka and rubber boots. "Sorry. Saw your car but I needed to finish feeding the beasts. Great to see you. Did Linda get you a drink?"

"She's a little busy," I said.

He threw the parka on the floor and kicked off his boots. The three dogs came bounding over to him. He raised his right hand a fraction of an inch and the dogs moved back across the room.

"I'm Gary. You must be Margaret."

"Sarah," she said.

"Margaret was my wife," I said.

"Wow, time warp or what. Sorry. Linda!"

"What do you want?" Linda yelled from the kitchen.

"Is the wine open?"

"You get it!"

"I'll just be a minute!" said Gary as he disappeared into the kitchen.

Gary came in carrying two plastic glasses and a bottle of sparkling Canadian wine. "You tried this yet? I've heard it's pretty good." He poured us each a glass, the wine foaming up and spilling on the plywood floor. "And you said I should put in the carpets." He handed us each a glass. Sarah stepped back to miss the drips.

"What about me?" said Keith from the floor.

"Ask your mother," said Gary.

Keith rolled off the beanbag and followed his father into the kitchen.

"Nice place," said Sarah.

"You get used to it."

"I doubt it."

Sarah wandered around the room, touching the arms of the chairs and sofa. Everything had dog scars, teeth marks, scratches. In front of the fireplace the plywood was ripped as if the dogs had tried to bury something. Sarah stopped at a cage full of wood shavings. I could smell the sharp urine smell from across the room.

"What's this?"

"I think the little girl has gerbils."

"Are they in there?"

"I think so." Sarah stuck her finger in the cage and rolled it across the wire bars and then jerked back. "Shit! The little fucker bit me!"

"Do you want to play with them?" said Janet, the six-year-old. She was standing behind me. "What's a 'little fucker'?"

"Never mind," I said.

Janet went to the cage. "Do you want to hold one? They're real cute."

"No. I'll take your word for it," said Sarah.

"Dinner's almost ready," said Linda. She walked over to Sarah. "I'm Linda."

"Sarah."

"I heard. Men are such idiots."

"Tell me about it," said Sarah.

"I thought we were going to eat," said Keith standing at the top of the stairs.

Janet ran to the doorway. "We're eating in here."

In the dining-room an ornate crystal chandelier hung over an old chrome kitchen table with a card table pushed against it. Paper plates were set along with plastic glasses and plastic utensils.

"Sorry," said Linda, "The dishwasher's still broken."

"What's for supper?" asked Janet.

"Just eat it," said Linda.

Gary carried in an aluminum tray of lasagna and placed it in the centre of the kitchen table. Keith reached across the table and scooped a huge gob of lasagna on his plate, licking his fingers as he sat back down.

"We don't say blessing around here. There's no time. Help yourself," said Gary.

"Looks great," I said. "Mind if I have some more wine?"

"Help yourself. That's what it's there for." I poured Sarah

and myself large glasses. Sarah reached across and took a tiny portion of lasagna and some Caesar salad from a large wooden bowl worn from the dishwasher.

"It's great you finally made it out. It's been almost what? Five? Six months?"

"It's been over a year."

"You've got to be kidding. How's painting?"

"Getting by," I said.

"Might have something for you. Another project."

"Good. I'm getting tired of kitchens."

"Yeah? Or the little housewives?" He winked at Sarah and took another portion of lasagna. Keith was finished his first helping. I hadn't even dished out my first.

"Get with it man," said Gary, "Eat it or lose it. I'll see if I can find another bottle of the bubbly. Time to celebrate."

Keith stood up and kicked back his chair. "This is stupid."

"Did you asked to be excused?" said Linda.

"Can I please be excused," said Keith as he bounded up the stairs.

"You're lucky you don't have kids," said Linda.

Keith reappeared at the top of the stairs wearing a parka.

"Where are you going?" said Linda.

"Nowhere," said Keith as he opened the back door and went outside.

Gary went into the kitchen. The doorbell rang and Janet ran to the door.

"Mom, it's the Puffy lady!"

"Well, let her in," yelled Linda.

A woman in her late fifties entered the house, nodding to us as she knocked the snow off her shoes. Linda looked up from her plate but didn't get up.

"We're just finishing up," said Linda.

"I didn't mean to disturb you. I was just in the neighbour-hood. Is Puff ready?"

"Janet, get Puff for Mrs. Smithers."

"Which one is Puff?" asked Janet.

"On the shelf. You know where."

Janet came back carrying a metal canister with Santa Claus and several reindeer printed on the side. "Puffy," said Mrs. Smithers. "This is wonderful. She so loved Christmas. I can put her under the tree. She always loved to sit under the tree with the presents at Christmas."

"I put her in a baggie so you can change canisters depending on the season," said Linda.

"That's lovely. How thoughtful," said Mrs. Smithers.

"How do you want to pay for Puff?"

"Can I pay you at the end of the month?"

"Gary! Mrs. Smithers wants to take Puff without paying."

Gary came out of the kitchen. "Hi Mrs. Smithers. Now we've discussed this before. You know you were to pay immediately after the cremation."

"But...."

"We cannot release Puff without payment. Maybe we'll just hang onto Puff for awhile."

"No, I need her for Christmas. Do you take cheques?"

"I'd rather not."

"Visa?"

"Visa will be fine, thank you. Linda, get a form for Mrs. Smithers."

"I need a drink," said Sarah.

I took Sarah's glass and went into the kitchen. On a shelf above the spice rack were seven metal canisters and several small plastic bags full of grey ash. I shook my head even though no-one was in the room. I couldn't help but think of accidentally knocking the ash off the shelf. Then what? 'Sorry, I just spilled your Dalmation.' I found the wine on the counter, refilled our glasses and went back to the table.

"Here's your receipt," said Gary. I handed Sarah her glass of wine.

"Thank you," said Mrs. Smithers. She opened the door and left. A fog of cold rolled in over the plywood floor.

I heard the sound of a skidoo starting up. Lights swung by

the front window and I saw Keith race past.

"He loves anything with a motor. Mopeds, motorcycles, skidoos, ATVs, dirt bikes—anything to propel him frantically within the confines of the acreage," said Gary. "At least he's not into drugs."

"Yet," said Sarah.

"Why don't you two go relax in the front room," said Linda. "Gary and I will clear things up and then maybe we can play some games or something."

"Great," said Sarah as we took our plastic wine cups into the front room. Janet put on a video and opened the gerbil cage. She took out the gerbils and lay on the plywood. The two young dogs lay beside her. The gerbils crawled over her and the dogs. On the television screen fish started singing underwater in huge clouds of swirling colour.

"Do you want coffee?" Linda's head appeared in the doorway.

"Yes. Thanks very much," smiled Sarah.

I nodded. Sarah's smile disappeared instantaneously.

"How long are we staying?"

"We can leave anytime. Whatever you want."

"I'm sure."

Linda came in with two chipped styrofoam cups of instant coffee, clouded with powdered creamer.

"Here you go. I added some creamer and sugar. I was running out of hands," said Linda.

"This is fine. Wonderful," said Sarah.

"Gary will only be a minute. Right, dear!"

"Be right there!"

"What about a game. I love games. Have you ever played Scruples? That's hilarious." The thought of Scruples with Sarah was painful.

"What else have you got?" I asked.

"Trivial Pursuit. What Trivial Pursuit have we got, Gary?"

"The one in the blue box. I'll be right there."

"Bring the wine! We also have Monopoly. Gary loves the buying and the selling."

We could try that," I said. Another compromise. Maybe that's how that game got to be so popular, a series of compromises through the decades. Maybe a couple of rum and cokes would assuage the night.

Gary came in with the bottle of Baby Duck. "Let's move the card table and get started," said Gary.

"Do you have any rum?" I asked.

"I'll see what I can do."

Linda retrieved the Monopoly game out of the stereo cabinet as Gary carried in the card table. Sarah and I moved in two chairs each and we were set. We sat down, dealt out the properties and I resigned myself to an evening of real estate tedium, a blur of rolling die, paper illusions, green plastic houses and red plastic hotels.

Scarf lay under the card table, his head resting on the plywood of the floor. He was nearly completely black and much larger than a normal Shepherd. Every so often the dog would look up and bare its teeth slightly. Gary said the dog was gentle, but the look was still sinister. A few years ago one of the pups had bitten me on the forearm. It didn't break skin but the bruise showed for a few weeks. The last time I visited I watched one of their trainers with a white arm brace get flipped over when Scarf bit down on the arm restraint. If I hadn't seen it myself I would have said it was impossible. Ever since then I had given Scarf an extremely wide berth.

Sarah watched Janet watch the video.

"Do you ever get slivers?" she asked.

Janet just looked at us with her eyes thin slits. She took a sip from her milk. I almost started laughing at her attempt to look menacing. In a few years she would be more successful.

The doorbell rang as the front door opened and a new German Shepherd came bounding into the front room, rebounding off our legs. She sniffed everything, tossing her head back and forth. A man and woman followed the dog into the house and stood at the front entrance.

"Gary! They're here!" Linda turned to the couple. "Is Mindy ready?"

"I think it's safe to say that," said the woman. "Hot and heavy."

Scarf looked up and then stood up and walked back into the other room.

"Shy?" said the man.

Gary dragged Scarf back into the living-room. "Might as well do it here. Too damned cold outside." He turned to us at the table. "You might as well keep playing. He'll only take a minute anyways."

"Whose turn is it?" asked Linda.

Scarf circled the female Shepherd, smelling her rear end. Mindy backed away and then backed into him, flipping her nose over her shoulder. She reminded me of the young girls in the Barbarian on Saturdays, flipping their hair out of their eyes. The two dogs circled in the middle of the room. Scarf manoeuvred behind Mindy but she moved away at the last minute. Finally he lifted his paws unto her back and mounted her. His tongue lolled out as he pumped into her.

Janet spilled her milk and the two young dogs licked up the milk as it dripped through the cracks of the floor.

Scarf arched his back and looked sheepishly at Gary as he pumped furiously into Mindy. Linda stood at the doorway with the couple. Sarah stared at me. I tried not to watch the two dogs humping by the table. Scarf yelped as he turned to dismount Mindy. Mindy started trotting around the room, dragging Scarf behind her. Mindy tried to rub Scarf off on the walls and then the edge of the sofa.

"His barb is still swollen," said Gary.

"You're kidding me," said Sarah.

"Prevents quick accidents. You know what I mean?" Gary nudged my shoulder. "There's another bottle of Baby Duck. Anyone feel like another glass?"

"Bring the bottle," said Sarah.

"Linda, you roll for me," said Gary from the kitchen.

Mindy lurched around the room trying to dislodge Scarf. She twisted and bucked. Scarf bounced along behind her, trying in vain to pull himself free. He yelped and looked up at Gary as he moved to the table with the wine.

"Don't look at me, pal. This is your ride. No pain, no gain."

"You always talk to your dogs?" asked Sarah. "They ever talk back?"

"They usually make more sense than people."

Mindy and Scarf brushed our legs as they moved into the kitchen. Scarf followed Mindy in a hop like action. At the doorway Mindy twisted and Scarf smashed against the door-frame before disappearing into the kitchen. Linda and Gary stood with the couple in the doorway.

"What if it doesn't take?" asked the man.

"It'll take. He's amazing. But if there is a problem bring her back and we'll have another go at her," said Gary.

"We should be so lucky," said the woman.

I turned away from Gary and Linda and the couple in the doorway. Sarah was staring at me.

"You fucked her, didn't you?" Sarah whispered.

"What are you talking about?"

"You know what I'm talking about. You fucked her didn't you."

"Who?"

"That woman when you painted her kitchen. Don't think I'm stupid."

The woman Sarah was talking about was 45 years old, single, separated or divorced I have no idea, with two kids. To Sarah that sounded romantic. To me I saw an overweight shrew who was always on my case about being too slow. I remember feeling an intense empathy for her husband who was probably still breathing a sigh of relief in his new locale as far away as humanly possible. To Sarah every human contact was a potentially sexual encounter. If only life was that simple.

"Was she good?" Sarah drained her wine glass and poured herself another. "Why did you fuck her?"

"I didn't fuck anyone...and keep your voice down."

"Why should I? You didn't have any respect for me. Why should I care?"

Gary opened the front door for the couple and a wave of cold air floated across the floor. The man called for Mindy. Scarf lay at Sarah's feet. The two dogs weren't on speaking terms anymore.

"My turn?" asked Gary.

"Mine. I'm buying two hotels. I'm going to bankrupt you. Next move."

"Good luck," said Gary.

"Can you pour me some more wine," said Sarah.

I stood up and moved to the window overlooking a field of snow, sparkling white in the darkness. Keith drove past in the skidoo, the motor sounding like an outboard. The headlights washed across the ceiling as he turned figure eights in the snow. He was dressed in his parka with a helmet and boots. He looked like a Canadian astronaut. Winter is our deep space.

"Why?" Sarah's voice was a hiss in my ear. She was standing beside me, a wine glass in one hand, a lit cigarette in the other.

"Listen, I didn't touch her. I didn't touch anyone. Do you want to leave?"

"No. I want to stay. Your friends are lovely."

I moved to the closet and got my jacket. "I need some air."

I walked out into the winter night. The air was almost solid and the cold bit into my skin. Keith turned the skidoo at the far end of the field, its thin light cutting into the darkness. I looked back at the house. Light spilled out onto the snow. Sarah was standing at the window, her arms folded across her chest. Scarf stood on his hind legs beside her.

NICHOLAS RUDDOCK works as a physician in Guelph, Ontario. He has also lived in Newfoundland, Quebec and the Yukon Territory. He has won prizes for both poetry and fiction, and his work has appeared in the Journey Prize anthology. The Canadian Film Centre has produced a film based on one of his short stories. His first novel, *The Parabolist*, will be published by Doubleday in February of 2010.

ALEX LESLIE was born in Vancouver. Her short fiction has been published in periodicals across the country, and has won a number of prizes including the CBC Literary Award. Her non-fiction won the gold medal for personal journalism at this year's National Magazine Awards. She is currently finishing work on a book of short stories. See alexleslie.wordpress.com.

JEFF PARK is an educator and writer who works in a variety of genres, including short fiction, poetry and drama. He has published a book on writing theory and narrative entitled *Writing at the Edge*, and recently completed a first poetry collection, *Living in the Flats and Sharps: The Jazz Poems*. He is currently at the University of Saskatchewan, where he teaches courses in writing, curriculum, literacy and English-language arts.

MARK ANTHONY JARMAN has published three collections of stories, *New Orleans Is Sinking*, *19 Knives* and *My White Planet*, and a travel book, *Ireland's Eye*. His hockey novel *Salvage King Ya!* is on Amazon.ca's list of 50 Essential Canadian Books, and he has won the Gold Medal at the National Magazine Awards. He is the fiction editor of *Fiddlehead* and teaches at UNB.